S0-ABA-299

The
Spyglass
Tree

THE SPYGLASS TREE

Albert Murray

Pantheon Books

New York

Library of Congress Cataloging-in-Publication Data
Murray, Albert.
    The spyglass tree/Albert Murray.
        p.   cm.
    I. Title.
PS3563.U764S69 1991
813'.54—dc20   90-53401
ISBN 0-394-58887-8

BOOK DESIGN BY CATHRYN S. AISON

For Mozelle and Michele

Bench

Marks

I

That many years later, the clock tower chimes you woke up hearing every morning were that many miles north by east from the sawmill whistles along Mobile River and Chickasabogue Creek, and the main thing each day was the also and also of the campus as it was when I arrived with my scholarship voucher and no return ticket that first September.

As you took your place in line with all the other freshmen waiting in the hallway outside the registrar's office that first Friday morning, there was a moment when you suddenly realized that you were actually on your own and you felt so totally all alone that it was almost as if everything that had happened before you came through the main gate (less than twenty-four hours earlier) and saw that many brick-red buildings with magnolia-white eaves and antebellum columns beyond the late summer green shrubbery with the rust-red dome of the dining hall against the bright blue preautumn sky was now already a very long time ago and in a place very far away.

But even so there was also the also and also of L & N express train whistles and creosote trestles, and the marco polo blue skyline mist that is always there when you remember the spyglass view from the chinaberry tree in the front yard of our three-room shingle-top shotgun house on Old Dodge Mill Road. Not to mention the tell-me-tale times around the fireplace and on the swing porch of the house itself. To say nothing of the long since hallowed lie-swapping and all of the ongoing good-natured woofing and signifying you had been permitted to witness outright or had otherwise contrived to overhear in places like Papa Gumbo Willie McWorthy's barbershop and on the veranda of Stranahan's General Merchandise store for that many years.

Another part of which was old Stagolee Dupas *(fils)*, the flashy-fingered jook joint piano player from New Orleans and elsewhere, with his custom-tailored jazz-back suits and hand-finished silk shirts and handkerchiefs and his deliberately pigeon-toed patent leather avenue walk and his poker-sly watchful eyes, in whose name and for whose sake Little Buddy Marshall and I had in time also come to do things that had nothing to do with playing music, just as I for my part had also already been cocking my all-purpose navy blue derring-do baseball cap and tightening my rawhide wristband like Gator Gus even when the situation I was in at the time had nothing at all to do with being the legendary money-ball pitcher he used to make you also want to be, along with everything else.

Yes, even as the copper-green sound of the vine-dampened reverberations—clinging and clanging over the huddled rooftops of the surrounding neighborhood—echoed across the rolling central Alabama farmlands and all the way out to the bright clay hills and the gray-green pine ridges of the outlying regions, took you back to storybook illustrations of medieval castles and cathedral towns, there was the also and also of Luzana Cholly and his twelve-string guitar and his 32-20 on a 44 frame and his sporty limp walk. Not only because old Luzana Cholly was the one who had once said what he said sitting under the L & N Railroad bridge at Three Mile Creek that time after he had caught me and Little Buddy Marshall trying to follow him and skip city on a northbound freight train and had brought us back as if by the nape of the neck and (for me at any rate) as if specifically to the door of Miss Lexine Metcalf's classroom—but also because of all the things Little Buddy Marshall and I had been daring and doing in his notorious name all along.

As for Miss Lexine Metcalf herself and her bulletin-board peoples of many lands, once she had singled you out, you were indelibly earmarked for Mister B. Franklin Fisher and his ancestral imperatives for the "talented tenth," to whom he said much had been given in raw potential, acknowledged or not, and from whom therefore much in commitment, development, refinement, and ultimate achievement would always be not only expected but required.

Nor were any of the essential implications of any of that diminished in any way at all by anything that I had found out by that time, about how everything had finally turned out for the self-same but perhaps not identical Little Buddy Marshall who always used to be there for daring and doing, before he decided to go where he went and tried to do what he always wanted to do.

Incidentally, I can't remember when Mama was not calling me Scooter because I can actually remember all the way back to the times when what she used to say was not really Scooter but Gooter. Which was probably all the way back during the time when I was still trying to crawl because what I remember her actually saying for Mama's little man was *Mama's yil man mamam yil gootabout man* and the way she always used to like to say bless his bones was *betchem bone betchem tweet bone*.

And when I was big enough to go outside the house and then the yard by myself, not only to play but also to run errands, she also used to say *Mama's little old scootabout man, lil old scootabout scatabout man out there amongst them. That's what he is. Out there scooting about all over the place. That's just exactly what he is. It what him im betchemtweet bone. With his little old sparkle-eyed buster-brown self and them nimble knees and twinkle toes just like little old Jack the Rabbit. Just like little old Jack the Rabbit in the briar patch, and Mama wouldn't trade him for a rich man's share in the Nettie Queen riverboat with that fifty-thousand dollar calliope.*

Once I came home from the first grade and Uncle Jerome the preacher, who was always christening or ordaining something, said what he said, and it was as if he was conducting one of his services. He stood up from the rocking chair, looking at me with his pulpit-solemn eyes and cleared his throat until his voice was ceremonial and placed his baptismal-firm hands on my shoulder as soon as Mama said, Mama's little scootabout man, he back home from all the way over yonder amongst them, he said, Now there's a name, notion, and designation to conjure with. Gentlemen, sir, as I am a witness.

Uncle Jerome may also have been the first one I ever heard talking about how secret messages from the abolitionists about the Underground Railroad used to be sent from plantation to plantation or by the grapevine. Because he was almost always there in the fireside crescent during midwinter yarn-spinning nights and he had his own rocking chair on the swing porch in the summer. In my case, you can bet that he was the one who wanted you to feel that Scooter was as much the code name for the fugitive slave zigzagging north by the Big Dipper as it was for Jack the Rabbit.

Whenever it was that I first heard about the Underground Railroad, by the time I had met Little Buddy Marshall at the pump shed the day after he and his family moved into the shotgun house diagonally across the street from Aunt Callie the Cat, it was as if I had been calling myself Scooter all of my life. In fact, I still can't remember ever calling myself anything else and I also said, That's what I'm supposed to be able to do, and he said, Hey you too, hey me too, man, you want to let's be good old buddies? And I said, Hey that's all right with me, man. So he said, I live right over there. So you want to come over to my house and I'll get my goddamn mitt and I also got a mask and a breast protector because I got to be a badass catcher, man, and I bat right-handed or left-handed, don't make no difference to me. And I told him I was supposed to be a big-league pitcher one of these days and that I got a regulation-size Spaulding glove that last Christmas.

He said, Hey call me Lebo, and before very long I also began calling him Skebo and then we began calling each other Skebootie because that was our way of saying that we were each other's buddies and that we were both bred and born in the briar patch. Which was also our stamping ground. Hey, shit, I reckon, man, he said. Hey, shit, I goddamn reckon.

II

You couldn't see the clock tower from your window but you knew it was on the women's dormitory across the mall on the other side of the dining hall and you also knew that the mall, which was also known as the lawn, was where the band pavilion was, and when you walked up the wide brick steps and across the main avenue to the white columns of the music school and stood looking back that way there were two other women's dormitories beyond the trees at the opposite end, and the main entrance to the dining hall was out to your right facing the clock tower, which was now out to your left.

The only part of the mall you could see from your window was the dome of the dining hall above the cluster of evergreens at the other end of the long four-story academic building that also completely blocked your view of the administration center and that part of the main campus concourse so that you couldn't even see the flagpole in front of the post office, which you knew was only one block away.

8

What you saw directly across the quadrangle was the corner of the near end of the academic building where the delivery trucks turned off for the service entrance to the dining hall, the campus laundry, and the power plant. You couldn't see any part of the laundry but you knew that the power plant was down the steep hill to your right because you could see the smokestack above the pine tops on the other side of the sophomore dormitory.

The water tank that is probably still the first campus landmark on the horizon after you turn off U.S. Highway 80 at the city marker on your way in from Montgomery and points north or south was all the way back to the left of your window and out of sight between the new science building where most of the academic class sessions were held at that time and the new gymnasium, which was also where dances were held and where concerts and plays were presented and movies were shown.

Back in those days the third floor of that dormitory was known as the Attic because the top half of the outside wall of every room slanted inward with the pitch of the rafters and also that was where the special freshmen students assigned to the upper end of the campus were quartered. But I liked everything about it as soon as I opened the door and saw that next to the window there was a door with a fire-escape landing outside.

As soon as my roommate came in, not more than fifteen minutes later, I liked him too. He was about two inches taller than I was and about ten pounds or so heavier. We had almost the same shade of brown skin, but his hair was coarse grain, almost straight, and almost glossy mat, and mine was soft, with a texture somewhat like moss and a sheen somewhat like steel wool.

He was wearing a tan corduroy sports jacket with khaki slacks and saddle oxfords and argyle socks, and he had opened the collar of his buttoned-down tattersall shirt, but he still had on his navy blue knitted tie. He also had a cloak-and-dagger trenchcoat slung over his shoulders and a tennis racquet tucked under his left arm.

Albert Murray

I said, Hi, and he put down his overnight bag and Hartman two-suiter, checking out the room in one ever-so-casual glance, and as we slapped palms Satchmo Armstrong style, he said his last name out of the corner of his mouth like a movie gangster. Then looking at me sidewise but with a conspiratorial twinkle he tucked in his chin like a musical comedy cadet and made a break as if to click his heels and added his first name and middle initial.

Then he said, Geronimo, which I guessed was a nickname meaning now you see me now you don't because whether you played cowboys and Indians or went to the Saturday shoot'em-ups, Geronimo was the chief who was forever escaping again (never mind that he finally ended up on the reservation—in his heyday he was one more badass Indian). Then it crossed my mind that the texture of his hair might mean that his family was part Indian, but I didn't say anything about that.

I said my last name, first name, and middle initial and we touched palms again but instead of my nickname I said Mobile, *seeing Bienville Square once more as you used to see the wrought-iron park benches and the splashing fountain and the tame squirrels when you stood waiting for the streetcar at the corner of Dauphine and St. Joseph with the Van Antwerp building against the sky and the waterfront only two blocks away.*

I also said Mobile County Training School, *seeing Blue Poplar Ridge again with the sky stretching away northward beyond the Chickasabogue and the flagpole above the flower circle and playground where the school bell scaffold used to be when I was in the primary grades,* and suddenly I felt a pang of nostalgia in spite of myself because I wouldn't be going home for the Christmas holidays. I couldn't afford the bus fare. Nor did I expect to be able to afford it for a visit next summer.

He said Chicago and named his high school and then he said that he had come to take courses in architecture and the building trades and that he intended to sneak in as many courses in history and literature as he could choose as electives or would get permission to audit. I said that I was there on a liberal arts scholarship grant but that I hadn't decided on my major and minor subjects yet because I still didn't know what I wanted to do with myself.

He pulled off his jacket and tie and on the way back downstairs to get his steamer trunk I told him that I was there by way of the Early Bird program, and that was when he began telling me about his great uncle (his mother's father's brother) called Old Sarge by some but who sometimes referred to himself in the third person as the Old Trooper and so now was widely known as Old Troop and sometimes addressed as Troop and as Trooper.

The Old Trooper was now in the business of backing entertainers and promoting prizefights but he would always also be one of the legendary Buffalo Soldiers from the old Tenth Cavalry Regiment with an endless repertory of tall tales and historical anecdotes and footnotes about the wild west in the days of Cochise and Geronimo and the Chiricahua Apaches. He had mustered out after the Spanish-American War, and at one time he had managed a cabaret for Jack Johnson and for a while he had also been part owner of a showcase theater on the T.O.B.A. (Theater Owners' Book Association, a.k.a. Tough On Black Asses) circuit and he had also underwritten baseball teams from time to time. One of the prizefighters he and two associates, one in Chicago and the other in Detroit, were backing at the moment was a very promising young heavyweight that I knew the *Pittsburgh Courier* and the *Chicago Defender* were already predicting would become a Jack Johnson and a Joe Gans all rolled into one.

On the way back from the dining hall that first Thursday night I found out that my roommate's family, including the Old Trooper, was really from Fort Deposit in Lowndes County, which was only about seventy-five miles away. As it turned out, it was the Old

Trooper who had financed my roommate's family's move north, where he finally settled in Chicago when my roommate was four years old.

Back inside the room again he stood looking around, and then he sat at his desk humming and whistling "Sleepy Time Down South" and "(Up a) Lazy River" and opened his lettering and sketch kits. Then he turned and said, How about this for a start and held up a card that was to be our personalized door plaque which he called our reversible escutcheon, giving me that sidewise glance with the movie gangster, conspiratorial twinkle again.

He had printed "Atelier 359" on both sides. But on one he had lettered CAUTION in red ink and in all capitals and then "work-in-progress" in lowercase, and beneath that there was a black-ink drawing of a hooded monk near the column of a cloister above a quill and a T square crossed over a Leyden jar. On the other side the word in all capitals was WELCOME and the lowercase phrase was "mischief afoot" and the drawing was of a satyr wearing a top hat playing a trumpet instead of Pan's pipes while cavorting on a keyboard that had a stem glass on his left and a cocktail shaker on his right.

I said, Hey, solid, Gates, and he looked around the room again and said, Not a bad pad, not great but okay for what we came to do, once we fix it up; and he started fixing it up as soon as he finished registration that next afternoon.

In those days there was an eleven o'clock curfew, and lights were supposed to be out at twelve, but that first night we went on talking in the dark until the wee hours, and that was when I found out that it was the Old Trooper who had decided to send him south for his first two years of college to get his bearings. Then he could transfer to any Ivy League or Big Ten university that he was eligible for. Or he could stay on in Alabama and get his bachelor's degree and then still go to the northern university of his choice for graduate studies.

That was also when he told me about how the Old Trooper had taken him around in the limousine to shop for his freshman wardrobe in the college department of the top men's stores in Chicago and when I told him that my Gladstone bag was my graduation gift from Miss Slick McGinnis in New York and that my cowhide looseleaf all-purpose notebook was from Miss Lexine Metcalf and my Elgin wristwatch was from Mister B. Franklin Fisher himself, I couldn't see him in the dark but I knew he was giving me that sidewise look again because what he said was, Heh, heh, haay, heh, heh, haay, and then I also guessed that he had turned his conspiratorial twinkle into a mock penny-dreadful chuckle because then he added, You too, roommate, you too, you too.

III

Miss Lexine Metcalf never did actually say what you were supposed to become or were on your way to becoming or even had already become another one of the very special bright-eyed little boys she was always on the lookout for but had found so precious few of over the years.

She herself didn't have to tell you anything because when the time came there were always plenty of others who had been doing so for her all along. All she had to do was show any special curiosity about you, and you were on the spot, and as soon as they felt that they had seen enough to tell that you were going to be the next one at long last, they began pointing and signifying as if it were all a classroom version of the old playground game in which you had been tagged as the one who was to be It.

Everybody knew that she always made it her very special personal business to know what the new crop of first-termers looked like on the very day school reopened each September. Then, some weeks before Maypole Day during your second-grade year, the speculation would begin about how well who would do next year when you finally made it to Miss Lexine Metcalf and her shawl of many colors and her magic blackboard pointers.

But before your classroom was the one with the globe stand and map rack and bulletin-board peoples of many lands and your front-row seat on the aisle next to the planting-box windows, there was first Miss Rowena Dobbs Singleton and second Miss Thelma Caldwell.

When Miss Tee took me through the double gate with the brick pillars and into the school yard that first Monday morning and we came on by the flagpole and the main building to the beginner's area, Miss Rowena Dobbs Singleton was the one who was there, because that was the room where everybody started, and she collected the slip that Miss Tee and Mama had filled out about me, and she said my last name and then my first name, and then my last name again.

Then you had to stand in line along the wall with all the other boys until she called your name again and showed you the table where your seat was and said, Boys and girls, this is the primer grade. This is the beginners classroom and I am the primer teacher and my name is Miss Singleton, Miss Singleton, repeat after me, Miss Singleton, again, Miss Singleton. Very good, very good, and now quiet, boys and girls, and she picked up her ruler and hand bell and said, Children, children, children, pay attention. Boys and girls who talk in class after the bell sounds will have to hold out their hand for lashes as punishment. Then she said, Answer present to your name, eyes forward, back straight like this. That is good posture. When you slump and slouch like a grumpy grouch, that is bad posture.

Miss Rowena Dobbs Singleton was also the first one to say, *Repeat after me, this is the way we wash our hands, wash our hands, wash our hands, this is the way we wash our hands so early every morning. This is the way we brush our teeth, brush our teeth, brush our teeth, this is the*

15

way we brush our teeth so early every morning. This is the way we brush our hair. This is the way we shine our shoes. This is the way we drink our milk. This is the way we raise our hands to recite and ask, repeat after me. May I not can I, may I, repeat, may I please be excused, Miss Singleton. And this is the way we stand and place our right hand over our heart when we say, repeat, I pledge allegiance to the flag and to the republic for which it stands one nation, indivisible, with liberty and justice for all.

This is A-B-C time. This is one-two-three time. These are letters. These are numbers, also numerals. This is the way letters from ABC through XYZ make words which is spelling. This is the way numbers go from one to ten which is counting, which is the way we find out which is more and which is less. This is the way we spell our name as written. This is the way we write our name as spelled. This is two ways we form letters to make words that form what we say which is writing and also, pay attention, printing. This is the way we say what we write which is reading, which is what storybooks are for. This is the storybook about Baby Ray (who lived in a somewhat but not altogether different place but not in a different time, not once upon a time but everyday, Baby Ray every day).

This is plus which is addition which is the way we do our sums to find more. This is minus which is subtraction. This is the way we take away and find the remainder. This is the way numbers tell us how much and how little and also how long and how short, how far and how near and how heavy and how light and on and on and on.

You were always supposed to sit in the same seat at the same table with the same tablemates, but sometimes everybody had to push all of the tables back and bring all of the chairs into a cozy family circle in the front of the room for story hour, and at other times, especially when the weather turned bad, everything was pushed against the walls to clear the floor for exercises and indoor games.

When you went to the blackboard, you were supposed to have your own eraser just as you were supposed to bring your own tablet, pencil, and wax crayons every day. But what you used at the blackboard was a piece of chalk from the box by the flower vase on the teacher's desk which is also where Miss Rowena Dobbs Singleton used to keep the little bell that she tapped for order. She kept the hand bell in the bottom drawer until she had to ring it for ten o'clock recess. Then she let it stay on the desk by the roll book until she rang it again at the end of playtime after lunch.

At each recess period, tablemates who put everything away and became tidy and quiet in the quickest time got to be the first in the boys' line on one side and the girls' line on the other to march out, and the best all-round tablemates for the whole day were the ones to line up first to go home at dismissal time.

In those days there were so many playthings and bright colors in Miss Rowena Dobbs Singleton's room that it was almost like a toy fair. But when you were promoted to Miss Thelma Caldwell for more spelling and the beginning of Elson readers and more addition and subtraction plus multiplication tables and short division and the beginning of long division and also of such simple fractions as the equal and unequal parts of whole pies and apples and sand tables, when you came into her room that next year that was where you sat in your first regular school desk with an aisle on each side and one seat mate (boys with boys and girls with girls) and two individual pen and pencil trays and inkwells plus an out-of-sight shelf for two book satchels and lunch boxes and also with hinged seats that you were always supposed to leave turned up like a theater seat when you went out for recess and at the end of the day.

Miss Thelma Caldwell also used to say, Boys and girls, and also, Dear children, and also, My dear darling pupils, and for a while you could still recite in chorus with the rest of the class as you had done when you had to repeat after Miss Rowena Dobbs Singleton, but before very long everybody was called on pupil by pupil and row by row, and when it was your turn and you heard the teacher-enunciated pronunciation of your officially registered

name once more you were supposed to stand in the aisle with your
shoulders square and your head erect and your eyes forward as if
the sunny blue sky outside the windows and the everyday working
hours sounds and echoes from the nearby neighborhood and street
vendors and the call of the wild territory beyond the tree line on
the other side of the rooftops of Chickasaw Terrace were not there
anymore.

Sometimes during those first two years you could hardly
keep from feeling sorry for yourself, not only during recitation and
blackboard example time, but even during recess periods. Then
when you were finally on your way home at last after the final bell,
you were free again for a while. But only until it was school-bell
time again the next morning until Friday afternoon and then next
Monday there would be week after week until Christmas holidays
and then beginning New Year's Day there would be month after
month until next May was over.

It was not that I didn't really want to become the buster-
brown schoolboy that Mama and Miss Tee had always said that I
was the one to be, nor was it that I was any less curious about all
that was going on around me in the classroom and out in the school
yard than I had ever been about so many other things up to that
time. That was the way Little Buddy Marshall was, not me. But
even so, school bells always sounded as sad as church bells tolling,
until I finally reached Miss Lexine Metcalf that following year and
she said what she said about all of the things that reading, including
map reading, was always all about.

She said opening books was like opening window shutters.
Which was also the beginning of what she always used to say about
books, including the newspaper and magazine clippings about
peoples of many lands on her bulletin board. It was also in her
classroom that you had to go up front to do map and globe
exercises as well as blackboard exercises. That was also why everybody could tell that you had advanced to Miss Lexine Metcalf just

by looking at you on your way to school, because that was the year when you could stop using your old oilcloth book satchel and strap your regular-size books crossways on your first-year geography book.

When you did something the way it was supposed to be done, Miss Lexine Metcalf always used to nod and smile and say, Very good, and call your name, and say, Very good, again; and when she was very pleased because you had done something that was very special because you had put more into it than was expected or required, she said, Excellent, superb, and put her fingertips together and touched them to her mouth and closed her eyes and then spread them and looked at you again and said, Yes, superlative.

Outstanding girls were wonderful young ladies and marvelous young ladies for whose sake princes also had to be charming no matter what else their ancestral mission required them to achieve. Outstanding boys were splendid young men, and when she called you one of her splendid young men it was precisely as if she were making you one of the Knights of her Round Table, which was no less real for being invisible.

Not that you didn't miss being outside anymore, especially when you looked out of the windows, because from my seat every time you stood up you could see northeast across the vocational workshop area to the poplar tree-line and the sky stretching away above that part of Chickasabogue Swamp and the L & N Railroad canebrake territory, nor was I quite ready to give up rambling and meandering with Little Buddy Marshall. But once Miss Lexine Metcalf was there for you Monday through Friday, I began to make up more and more excuses not to play hooky to do so.

The first time she said who if not you was before class one Wednesday morning. I was there that early because I wanted to have the globe and map rack all to myself while everybody else was either still on the way or waiting and playing around outside until the first bell for the flag formation. When she looked up from her desk and saw me coming in as I had asked permission to do, she said, How conscientious you are, a young man with initiative, and why not, because who if not you.

Who indeed? she said the next time, which was the day I stayed after school because I wanted to read the new bulletin board display all by myself and the time after that was the day I stayed in during the first part of the noon recess to work on my cutouts for the new sand-table project, and when I came out to the playground Simon Ray Hargroves saw me and came up and whispered, Hey, Scooter, boy you better watch out, man, you mess around and let old lady Metcalf get her claws on you and she ain't gone never let you alone. He was whispering not only because he was being confidential but also because you're not supposed to use nicknames on campus. You could get demerits for that, just as you could for keeping your hands in your pockets and wearing your cap crooked or backward.

Not as long as you were at Mobile County Training School, he said, and I said, Not me, man, and he said, Well, you sure better watch out then, because everybody knows she always been dead set on finding somebody so she can help old man B. Franklin Fisher hook him and turn him into a mad genius. Man, before long she going to be giving you a whole stack of extra work and stuff just to see how much more you can do and the more you do, the more she going to keep piling on and piling on.

Which by that time she had already begun doing and was to continue to do right on up through each succeeding homeroom teacher until it was time to turn me over to Mister B. Franklin Fisher himself for the Early Bird program, reminding me all the while that some are called and some are not.

And some are also called, she also used to say, and heed not. She said, Some are called to the church, some to the bedside, some as advocates to the bar of justice. While I myself am called to the classroom. Who can tell just what you might be called to do, my bright-eyed young man. For all we know, you may have to travel far and wide just to find out what it is you are called for.

When I came out onto the play area late during another noon recess period, the first one to spot me was Jaycee Robinson from Chickasaw Terrace and he said, Boy, I'm telling you, pretty soon you ain't hardly going to be able to make it out here at all no more. Boy, look to me like she just about got you right where she want you already, and I said, That's what you say, man. That's what you say.

Because by that time I was absolutely satisfied that she was always going to make sure that I got outside in plenty of time to join in whatever games they were playing that day, because sometimes I used to sneak glances back up at the window and find her peeping down to see how well I was making out.

I said, That's all right about some old lady Metcalf, man. I said, Come on, let's go, Jaycee, man. I got your old lady goddamn Metcalf swinging, man. I didn't say what you mean *old* lady Metcalf, because everybody knew that she was hardly even thirty yet, but I also knew that as far as most grade-schools pupils during my time at Mobile County Training School were concerned, it was as if she didn't have any business being that young and good-looking and wearing such stylish clothes to boot if she was also going to be that book smart and that serious about everything anyway, although she was just as nice as she was strict. When a lot of them had to say something about her, they always made it sound as if they were talking about a middle-aged nun from the Saint Francis Charity Hospital.

I said, Man, don't worry about no Miss Lexine Metcalf. I said, She promised my big auntie to keep a special eye on me, so you know what that mean. But I wasn't about to tell him anything at all about how I always felt when she used to say, You will go where you will go and you will see what you will see, so you must learn what you must learn because who, if not you, will do what you must do, my splendid young man.

IV

The monument that marked the site of the original campus—the original log cabins of the old slave compound—had been in place for some twenty-odd years. It had a triangular base that supported three bronze men, the one on the right holding a seed in one hand and a hoe in the other, the one on the left with a hammer and an anvil, and the one in the center seated with an open book on his knee, and not only had it been the most famous landmark on the campus ever since it was dedicated, it had also become one of the national emblems of Afro-American aspirations and achievement through education.

In the classroom that first Monday morning with my chair facing in from the wall of shoulder-high windows toward the lectern and the blackboard because that way you could see the back row without having to turn and look behind you, and with everybody hushed and waiting to hear and see whose name came next, and with the hailing and chattering back-on-the-scene voices coming and going down along the walks and hedges outside and with the back-to-work sky music of delivery truck horns and motors grinding and rumbling and honking in the distance beyond the nearby tempo of the neighborhood traffic humming and buzzing and beeping back and forth along the campus thoroughfare, I said what I said. I said, Here, meaning not only here as in present in the flesh on the spot as of now as against absent and thus not here but elsewhere. I said, Here, meaning not only as prescribed and thus required by attendance codes and regulations but also as promised on my own in all sincerity and thus here above all as in partial fulfillment of that which has long since been intended.

Because even as I said it I was thinking, Me and my own expectations me and also the indelibility of the ancestral imperative to do something and become something and be somebody. Then when the instructor finished checking the roster and opened the textbook and held up the blackboard pointer for attention it was precisely as if he were about to say and one and two and three and four and so forth and so on and onward.

The campus was inside the corporate limits of the township that it was named for, but it was also almost like another complete town in itself, with its own surrounding communities and satellite neighborhoods. The main grounds added up to about 145 acres at that time, and the tree-lined avenue that ran from the dormitories near the academic quadrangle and curved and sloped all the way past the trades school workshops and ended on the low hill known as the ag side just about one mile long. Then there were some three thousand more acres of cultivated fields, orchards, and fenced-in livestock ranges.

It had all begun back at the end of the post–Civil War period known as the Reconstruction when it was a makeshift elementary school for freedmen and their families. The first classrooms had been in a cluster of stick-and-dirt cabins in one of the old slave compounds on the old Strickland plantation, some of which was still owned by contemporary Stricklands who were still among the most powerful people not only in the county but in the central part of the state.

The founding fathers, three former fugitive slaves also known as the Triumvirate—a fieldhand, a blacksmith, and a handyman—who had escaped to the North to join the Union army eighteen months before Lincoln issued the Emancipation Proclamation and had in exchange for various personal chores during free time in camp between battles been given elementary-lessons in reading, writing, and arithmetic by Yankee soldiers, some officers, some enlisted men, some abolitionists, some just plain Billy Yanks willing to make a swap.

After Appomattox, which ex-slaves almost always referred to as Surrender, the three of them worked their way back from Virginia to Alabama with the express and unwavering purpose (however vaguely defined at the outset) of initiating their own local Reconstruction program even as other ambitious freedmen here and elsewhere sought to achieve, exercise, and safeguard the rights to full citizenship provided for in the Thirteenth, Fourteenth, and Fifteenth Amendments, by going directly into politics as such, some as local, state, and even national office-seekers, and some as agitators and organizers.

They had begun as sharecroppers, with their own mule, plow, two-wheeled ox carts, jerry-built wheelbarrows, credit for seeds, fertilizer, rations, hand tools, and farming implements at the Strickland commissary plus an option to buy their first forty acres on an installment plan, and before very long they had the beginnings of a school that was to become an attraction for students not only from all over the state and region but also from across the nation at large, so much so that as the names on so many of its buildings indicated, it also attracted a considerable amount of financial assistance from such movers and shakers as Collis P. Huntington, John D. Rockefeller, Andrew Carnegie, and numerous others who regarded it as a pioneering effort in post–Civil War education.

In the early days all students were required to work for room, board, and tuition. There were no entrance fees or incidental charges. Those who could afford to pay were directed to the contributions office where they were given forms requesting their parents to become subscribers to the ongoing campaign for funds. But no student could pay in lieu of work and every student was also required to learn a trade in addition to whatever courses you chose as your primary vocation.

The first two generations of students were summoned to and from field, shop, and classroom alike by the same old bell that had once regulated life on the plantation before the war, and they planted and processed the food they ate. They produced and marketed such farm products as chickens, eggs, dairy products, and also livestock. They also cut the timber for lumber and they made the bricks and constructed the buildings that were to house them, and in the process they also learned to build and furnish their own houses, provide for their families, and develop or improve their communities wherever they settled.

Nor was there any end to the tasks early members of the faculty, whose dedication is a story in itself, had to perform. They had to be artisans, husbandmen, and tradesmen as well as classroom instructors. They had to be church workers as well as health and hygiene missionaries. They had to be fund-raisers combing the country for benefactors and able to convince many of the toughest captains of commerce and industry that by making generous donations to the school they were doing far more than underwriting the education of the children and grandchildren of slaves. They were investing in the future of the reunited United States as a great twentieth-century nation among the other great nations of the world, not in such direct words to be sure, but that was the point they put across.

Anecdotes and details about all of that were very much a part of the indoctrination that your orientation sessions during that first week were all about. And you were also to hear it again as the "gospel of Afro-American uplift," not only during the annual commemoration ceremonies that next spring, but also in allusions and quotations by almost every speaker who addressed the general student assembly on any official occasion.

V

I can still see myself at the long corner table by the rubber plant in the southeast wing of the main reading room on the second floor of the library, from which you could see part of the gymnasium through the poplar branches outside the windows that also over-looked the traffic circle and the lot where the visiting athletic teams parked their buses.

When you stood up you could also see the ticket shack and the admission gate to the athletic field which was out of sight down the hill. Beyond the high fence a few feet off the right of the vehicle entrance you could also look down onto the tennis courts at the other end of which you could also see the red-brick two-story residence of the dean of men at that time, and in the distance beyond the fence line and scrub-oak thicket there was the open sky above the sweet-gum slopes and the pine ridge somewhere south of Montgomery Fork.

As often as not when there was an assignment with a set of factual details to be looked up, I also used to work for a while at another long table near the open reference shelves at the other end of the main reading room and from there you could see across the thoroughfare to the back entrance to the administration building and the front columns of the old academic hall, and there was also the traffic along all of the walks in the academic area also known as the upper end.

Every time I looked down from that end of the library and saw all of the other students coming and going between class bells during those first weeks of that first fall term, I felt that old pang of isolation you often get when it hits you that you're in a place that you're not yet used to. But I didn't feel lost because I also felt how lucky I was to be there and because I was so excited about all of the things I woke up every morning hoping that I was getting that much closer to. It was enough to make you cross your fingers, and every time I remember how often I used to do just that, I still feel very lucky all over again.

But my usual place in the reading room from the very outset was the table in the corner where the rubber plant was, and this many years later I can still see the chalk white lines against the red clay tennis court and the green-stained bleachers as they were in the late summer sunshine and sometimes also in an early mid-September shower while I was reading about the role of the bards, scops, and gleemen in the evolution of language and literature in England, and also about the origin of civilization in Mesopotamia and about the culture of Egypt and about the Nile Valley and the ancient dynasties.

Along with what I was reading later on about the decline and fall of Rome into the Dark Ages and about the coming of medieval times, and along with English literature from Chaucer through Sir Thomas Malory and also along with selected freshman classics for the Introduction to Ideas and Literary Forms, there was the central Alabama Indian summer outside with the leaves turning from late September green to October yellow mixed with scarlet before becoming mostly shades of the tans and browns and brownish grays of harvest fields and game-bird feathers.

Nothing has ever surpassed the coziness of that corner of the reading room as it was when the first frost came that year. And then in a few weeks it was November and most of the trees were beginning to be bare and the thermometer outside had begun to drop below fifty degrees and then below forty, and inside it was as if you could smell the warmth from the radiators along the walls, but it was really the furniture polish and the liquid floor wax and there was also that trace of stamp-pad ink and binding glue and cataloging-room shellac that almost always used to be there when you used library books.

But before all of that and also before the gauze-thin tree whispering showers beyond the soft steady rattle of the drain pipes, there were those bright days during the first weeks of that September when all of the windows were open and along with the maps and illustrations spread out on the table in front of me there was a spicy smell of recently cut hedges and lawn grass and you could also hear the tennis balls being plipped and plopped and the voices of the referees and sometimes also a smattering of applause.

Then one afternoon I realized that for some time what I had been hearing was only a very casual plipping and plopping, plipping and plopping of fewer and fewer balls back and forth with no referee calls and no applause, because that many weeks of fall-term class sessions had come and gone along with that many social events including the first two home football games and also that much time hanging out on the Strip and in the radio lounge off the main stem, and I also realized that I already knew why I felt the way I felt about being where I was.

In the classroom you were a student among other students and you did what you did among them and along with them and sometimes together with them, not only as in roundtable discussions, seminars, and laboratory and workshop exercises, but even when you were responding to a direct question from the instructor, you were participating in a group session and as such you were also always reacting to and interacting with other members of the class.

But as soon as you came into the library it was almost always as if you were all alone and on your own again, not that you were ever really unaware that you were still actually surrounded by that many other students, faculty, and staff, and also visitors and sightseers. But even so it was very much as if everybody else was there to be an incidental part of what a college campus and a college library were really supposed to be.

Not only that, but what with the biggest globe (revolving on a tilted axis) I had ever seen, and what with all of the maps and atlases and mileage charts along with all of the books and documents and pictures and relics and artifacts only that many short steps away, it was also almost as if you had a sand table of the whole world always all to yourself.

My roommate went to the library mainly to browse through the current newspapers and magazines every Monday, Wednesday, and Friday, mostly during free time in the midafternoon; and sometimes he would also go back again for a while on Saturday morning.

In those days the periodicals room was on your left as you came into the main lobby and you could usually find him by himself at the same table in the corner near the shelves where the technical journals were, but he always began with the big city newspapers. Then he would go through the *Saturday Review of Literature* and then the weekly news magazines and then the monthly and quarterly reviews.

When you saw him up in the main reading room, which was not often and never for very long, sometimes he would be in the open reference section making notebook entries at one of the wall tables where the high chairs were. But usually he went straight to the card catalogs section at the main circulation counter, and when he found what he wanted he checked it out and did all of his reading back in 359, sometimes sitting with his leg folded under him in the sea captain's chair that he had picked up from somebody in the furniture repair shop in the industrial arts area, and with the book tilted in front of him on the adjustable drafting board, sometimes with the chair turned so that he could rest both legs across the bed.

But most often he liked to read sitting propped up in bed with the book on his thighs, sometimes smoking one of his fancy pipes which he never took outside the room and sometimes not. But always with a pencil behind his ear and his notebook within easy reach.

The sketches, blueprints, and watercolors on the wall behind the head of his cot and near the drafting table were his own work. Some were class assignments but most were field sketches ripped from his $8\frac{1}{2}'' \times 11''$ grid pad and thumbtacked up as mementos that sometimes became entries in his ever-present notebook, which he kept like a sea captain's log and sometimes called his daybook and clay book and clue book, his testament and also his doomsday book of portable property which he used to refer to as the goods not only in the sense of canned, packaged, and dry goods and other provisions for a survival kit, but also in the sense of getting and thus having specific inside information or evidence about something.

Incidentally, in no time at all you could almost always tell when he was about to reach behind his ear for his pencil for another entry, because he would either move directly back from what he was reading, or stand back from whatever he was inspecting and give it his sidelong stare and close his eyes for a moment, or he would rub his hands as if licking his chops and go into his heh-heh-heh imitation of the mustache-twirling, lip-smacking villain of the penny-dreadful pulp story, but then instead of actually saying ah-ah and all of that, he used to say, Yeah, verily.

As soon as I saw and heard him do that the first time, I could tell that it was something he probably always did because it reminded me of what Little Buddy Marshall always used to do. Whenever he was about to have to take a chance on something, old Little Buddy Marshall always used to tilt his head to one side and close his right eye and squint like a poker player, studying his cards through the haze of smoke curling up from the cigarette dangling from the corner of his mouth. Then he would suck his teeth two times and say, Hey, mighty right, hey, goddamn right. Hey, shit I reckon.

When something was good or even outstanding to Little Buddy Marshall, it was either some great shit or some bad shit. So when he judged something to be no good he used to say, Man, that shit ain't going to stack. Man, ain't nobody going to tell me you can make some old thin-ass shit like this stack. Man, I bet you my bottom goddamn dollar. Man, I'm telling you. This shit come from running off at the goddamn bowels. I don't care what nobody say. Because I know good and goddamn well what the goddamn fuck I'm talking about. I'm talking about you looking at some shit that ain't shit and then I'm talking about something you can put your money on.

Anytime Little Buddy Marshall used to say, Hey, shit, I reckon, it meant that he was ready to take a chance on something, sometimes even regardless of the consequences. But it was not very long before I realized that when my new roommate said, Yeah, verily, you never knew when he was also going to say, But, on the other hand. Not that he was less willing to take chances. He was even more of a gambler and a rambler than Little Buddy Marshall ever even dreamed of being. But the chances he took were more a matter of calculated risk. Whereas I always knew that Little Buddy Marshall took many more things for granted than I myself ever did.

VI

After lights out most nights I used to talk to him about Gasoline Point and Mobile; he asked about the Gulf Coast and about the bayous and sandbars and canebrakes; he also wanted to hear what I knew about Creoles and Cajuns, and I said I knew much more about Creoles than about Cajuns, but that I did know some and I had been to Chastang and Citronelle, which Gasoline Point people always used to think of as Cajun settlements.

He wanted to know which Indians, if any, I had grown up hearing the most about, and I said, The Chickasaws, the Choctaws, the Seminoles, and the Creeks, and I said, Especially the Creeks because from as long ago as I could remember, any time you saw somebody in Gasoline Point with very dark skin and coal-black straight or somewhat wiry hair, it was almost always said that whoever it was belonged to a family with blood mixed with the Creek Indians.

That was something you knew about just as you had always known about how Uncle Jo Jo the African and the people who had originally settled on African Baptist Hill and also founded African Baptist church had come through middle passage in the old Clotilde in August of 1859.

I said, Naturally you were always used to seeing Creoles and Cajuns, Choctaws, Chickasaws, Creeks, and Seminoles along with Cubans, Puerto Ricans, Mexicans, a few gee-chee-talking West Indians and a whole lot of others during Mardi Gras every year, not only in the parades but also on the sidewalk all along the route of the procession.

As close as Gasoline Point was to the waterfront of a seaport town like Mobile, you also grew up used to seeing ships from the seven seas flying flags of many lands. And just as you were used to knowing which downtown stores sailors and merchant seamen gathered around and also what points on which downtown side-streets were mainly Cajun or Creole or Cuban, you also knew that when you came toward the foot of Government Street and approached the area of Commerce Street and Water Street, you were always going to hear sailors and shopkeepers speaking more foreign languages than you could identify.

When I told him about Luzana Cholly, he filled me in some more about the Old Trooper. He had mustered out in 1900 and settled in California for a while, had first met Jack Johnson when Old Jack was out there building up the reputation that was to lead to the heavyweight championship of the world in the next five years.

The night club deal was a few years later in Chicago, he said, and I said, Hey, so the Old Trooper was still in during the Spanish-American War. So was his outfit in there with Teddy Roosevelt's Rough Riders? And he said, Well, not exactly. Old Troop was in the Tenth and they were right there with the Rough Riders in that action on San Juan Hill all right. But you know something? They went up that son-of-a-bitch *on foot,* because their horses were still in the Port of Embarkation back in Florida.

That was one of the Old Trooper's one thousand plus one tall tales for later, he said. But actually it came up again sooner than later because within a week or so, we found out that there were some of the Old Trooper's saddle buddies from the Tenth and also from the Spanish-American War along with veterans from the Ninth and quite a few not so old doughboys from the AEF right there on the campus, not only on the dean of men's staff and in the trades school, but also in the academic department, and also the music department.

The first time he ever mentioned anything at all about his father was when he said what he said the night that I told him that Mama and Papa had moved from the old plantation country up in Escambia County where I was born down to the shotgun house on Dodge Mill Road during the wartime shipbuilding boom. He said, when they moved from Lowndes County to Chicago, it was part of the postwar boom, and that was when he also said that his father didn't make it back from overseas, and that was why the Old Trooper had come down and taken the family back to live with him.

I didn't get to know my natural father, he said, because I was not quite two years old when he went to camp. And then he said, so the father whose name I bear is really only a man in a photograph. Three photographs all posed in a studio, one as a young sport, one with his bride, and one in uniform. You know, wraparound leggings, tight coat with stand-up collar, and overseas cap.

That was why I decided to tell him about Miss Tee, something I had never brought up on my own with anybody before. Not even Little Buddy Marshall. I had said what I said to him because after Miss Minnie Ridley Stovall did what she did at Mister Ike Meadow's wake that night while everybody thought I was asleep, I knew people were going to be whispering and I didn't want him to think that I didn't know what was going on.

I didn't say anything about that part of it, but I did tell him that I had never been able to bring myself to ask Miss Tee anything whatsoever about how it all had happened. I had to pick up as much as I could without letting anybody know that I was even curious, and in due time I found out that she had had to leave boarding school and she couldn't face her family and neighbors back in her hometown, so that was why I happened to be born in Escambia County. She had an older cousin who had finished the same boarding school several years earlier and was teaching down there. It was this cousin who was the one who took her in and also arranged for Mama and Papa to adopt me.

But I never did find out anything at all about who my father was, I said, because she was the only one in Gasoline Point who knew. And man, I just have never been able to say anything to her about any of it. And that's when he said, Man, fathers. Just wait until you hear some of the riffs and hot licks I've been grooving and running on fathers all these years. And uncles, too, he said. Not to mention mothers, aunts, godmothers, and some others.

VII

When I stopped off in the lounge on my way back alone from the dining hall one night about three weeks into that first September, there were three freshmen and four upperclassmen with their chairs pulled up in a semicircle around the radio console. But they were not really listening to the program of recorded music that filled in the thirty minutes before the news and sports broadcasts. They were listening to each other, with the music which I call downtown department store pop songs—"Smoke Rings," "Isn't It a Lovely Day?" "The Little Things You Used to Do," or "I Only Have Eyes for You"—and instrumentals, in the background like the wall furnishings.

It was a session about what your roommate was really like, and they were mostly just joking, and I found a spot for my chair; and when my turn came, I said what I said and that was how I became the one who was actually responsible for the nickname my roommate was to be known by, although I didn't have that name or notion or any other nickname in mind at all.

Later on I would have said he was by way of becoming a polymath, but I don't think that word was current then. But I had just read the captions to the illustrations of Christopher Marlowe's play *The Tragical History of Dr. Faustus* in my anthology of English literature, so I said, Doctor Faustus, and when somebody said Doctor Whostus, I said, You know about that guy that made the big deal to swap his immortal soul with the Devil, and one of the upperclassmen said, Oh yeah, him. Oh yeah, goddamn, hey yeah, that's a good one. And before anybody else could open his mouth, I realized that they were all thinking about the magicians we had all seen come on stage wearing a top hat and a frock coat and also a black cape with a red lining and carrying a cane and begin by announcing themselves as diabolical craftsmen and technicians who had sacrificed their souls to the devil in exchange for knowledge of forbidden secrets of the universe.

Which made him a witch doctor in a top hat. So somebody said, Snake doctor. Which in a day or so had been reduced to snake as in snake-oil salesman to be sure, but also, and indeed precisely, as in snake in the grass. Because in a week or so even those who were in on the session in the lounge that Thursday night and so had to know that my main point about Doctor Faustus was that my roommate wanted to study and master the entire curriculum seemed nevertheless to have come to take it for granted that a sneaky snakiness was what his sidelong smile and chuckle and his ever-so-casual and offhand manner were really about.

Nor according to some could anything be a sneakier game of one-upmanship than his classroom deportment. He always sat in the back row with his chair tilted against the wall as if he were totally preoccupied with something other than the discussion under way, and when he was called on to recite he always looked up from whatever he was reading, writing, or sketching as if surprised, but he always answered as if he had heard what everybody else had said from the outset. Not only that, but with his quietly conversational responses he not only upstaged everybody else, but also began a brief dialogue with the instructor. Then he would tilt his chair back again as if nothing had happened.

Faust, Faustus, or Snake Doctor, it was all the same to him, he said when I told him about how it all had gotten started in the lounge that Thursday night. But you could tell that he was very pleased at the way it had turned out, so I asked him what he thought a name like that would do for his reputation among the coeds, and he rubbed his palms and knuckles and went into his mock penny-dreadful heh-heh-heh.

They may be academic chuckleheads who are here only to acquire a means for more bread and circuses, he said, but this matter of sobriquets does have pragmatic implications which in this case shall be assayed anon.

And assay he did before the end of the next week and he found out that the Snake had already achieved such notoriety in the girls' dormitories and that getting dates was not going to be a problem. Not that either one of us was ready to take on a regular girlfriend yet. I had decided that all of that would have to come later, and I couldn't afford it anyway. After all, I was not even sure that I was going to be able to come up with the minimum amount of cash you needed for academic incidentals. So money for date favors and treats definitely was out of the question for me.

He could spare the spending change but for the time being he was even less willing to put in the hours you had to spend shucking and stuffing and jiving in the dining hall and on the promenade mall than I was. As a matter of fact, we both decided that we didn't even want to be *invited* to escort anybody to a dance or any other social function, not even entertainment series movies, concerts, and plays, to which admission was by Student Privilege card.

You couldn't be too careful about things like that. Or so they used to say in those days. And he had also been warned by his mother and the Old Trooper among others in Chicago as I had been told time and again by Mister B. Franklin Fisher and Miss Lexine Metcalf among other well-wishers down Mobile way, including the one and only Miss Slick McGinnis, that some coeds came to college to earn a degree but that the certificate that some others were out to get just might be one with *your* name on it.

So Snake was just the name for the game we both had in mind for the time being, and he made the most of it, and so did I. Because it faked quite a few of the more adventurous coeds into taking him on as a city slicker from the big up-north city of Chicago, and as his roommate I was automatically credited with, or accused of, being his buddy from the down-home city of Mobile.

I heard about you, a sophomore whom I will not name but who was from Birmingham and was taking Elementary French Review No. I, said as we were coming out of class one day. I heard all about you, you and that roommate of yours, the Snake. And I said, You can't go by what you hear, and before she could say anything, I also said, The best way is to find out things for yourself, and she said, Aw—you go on now, boy. But when she gave me a playful shove, I caught her hand and she said, What you think you doing, freshman? And I said, Being very fresh and very, very mannish, and she said, See there, what I heard was true. I was still holding her hand and I said, I hope so the way you signifying.

There was also the one who was a junior, no less, from Pittsburgh. She worked in the library and sometimes she was the one at the main circulation desk and after several weeks I could tell she was curious about me and I thought it was because of all the time I was spending at the table in the corner by the rubber plant. So as good-looking as she was, I pretended that I didn't really see her even when she was the one stamping the checkouts. But then one day she said what she said and that was the beginning of that.

You sure had me fooled, she said, and I said, Who me? How? and she said, Here I was thinking that you were kinda cute to be such a bookworm and come to find out you're rooming with the Snake of all people, and I said, What's wrong with that, and she said, He's so stuck on himself he goes around acting like he's God's gift to women, and I said, I'll settle for being God's gift to you, and she said, Well if you aren't the freshest freshman yet. So when her regular boyfriend went on trips with the football team and then the basketball team, she was the one.

That was the kind of on-campus action my roommate and I had going for us that first year, and I still don't know how I got away with it all without ever being called Little Snake or Snake Two or Snake Number Two or the Lizard or the Eel or something like that. Somebody was forever saying that we were two of a kind, but I was known as but not addressed as the Other One.

So much for Doctor Faustus as far as just about everybody else was concerned. But as pre-sophomoric as it probably sounded to an upperclassman coming as it did from a newly arrived freshman, I still think it was a pretty good analogy because what I really meant was the fact that my roommate was the first student I ever met who really believed that everything you studied in a classroom should become just as much a part of what you did everyday as everything else. To him, nothing was just academic stuff, so as far as he was concerned, there was no reason whatsoever why you shouldn't know just as much about the fundamentals of any course in the curriculum as any student who had checked it as the major for a degree. After all, as he had already said as he unpacked his books, the very best undergraduate courses were only a very brief introduction to some aspect of the plain old everyday facts of life that were just as important to you as to anybody else.

Which is why you never knew what his side of the room was going to look like when you came back at the end of the day. Or, for that matter, sometimes when you woke up in the morning. As often as not, the drafting board would be flattened out into a work table and rigged up with whatever equipment he'd have come by for whatever exercise he had underway. One day it might be a makeshift chemistry laboratory. The next day it might be set up for a problem in physics or biology, and when he was reviewing some historical period, he sketched his own maps, and he always got a special kick out of making his own war room mock-ups and outlining the strategies and retracing the maneuvers of the crucial battles of the great army and naval commanders.

During the second week of classes he had picked up the footlocker now under his bed from a senior in the building trades and that is where he stashed his special equipment, including not only his drafting kit and surveying and mapping instruments, but also his 16-mm camera, binoculars, and the parts he was already accumulating by mail order for the amateur radio set and the model airplane he was to build and operate from time to time that next spring.

Meanwhile, by the middle of October he had begun a window greenhouse project that he always found time to keep going full swing no matter whatever else came up. It started with two baskets of ferns he brought in from the greenhouse out on the ag side and hung above the books on the ledge that he also used as an extension of his work corner. Then a few days later he filled in the rest of the space with two shelves of terra-cotta pots, and before the end of November a fine growth of English ivy, tiger aloe, gold dusk, and silver dollar jade was underway, and by the time that first winter settled in, there were red geraniums and yellow nasturtiums, and deep purple African violets in blossom.

Each plant specimen was tagged with its Latin label, but when he got around to adding orchids he called them his Nero Wolf project. So the day I came in and he looked around from what he was probing wearing a pawnbroker's eye piece, I started laughing and I said, Hey man, goddamn. Don't tell me you're a jewel thief, too, and he said, Touché, old pardner, and laughed along with me. Then he said, But what about Sherlock and his magnifying glass and what about Benvenuto Cellini the goldsmith and his loupe? Not that the cat burglar doesn't have his challenges for the likes of the old Snake. Hey hey haay, roommate. It's a thought. Good thinking, roommate. Good thinking.

VIII

There was a time when everybody in Gasoline Point had expected Creola Calloway to go out on the circuit and become a world famous entertainer. Even before she was thirteen years old, people were already talking about how every vaudeville company that came to play in Mobile in those days always tried to hire her, always promising to make her a headliner in no time at all.

Nobody doubted it. Her endowments were all too obvious. She was so good-looking that she made you catch your breath, and when it came to doing the shimmie-she-wobble, the Charleston, the mess-around, or any other dance step, including ones made up on the spot, she always took the cake without even seeming to try, and also without making anything special of it afterward.

By her fifteenth birthday most people seemed to have decided that her fame and fortune were only a matter of time and choice, which they took for granted would be any day now. Not that anybody ever tried to rush things. After all, along with all of the fun they had enjoyed speculating about her possibilities, there was also the fact that Gasoline Point would not be the same without her.

As for myself, once I became old enough to begin to realize what they were talking about, I couldn't ever think about her leaving without also thinking of her coming back, and what I always saw was her rearriving with her own road company and own chauffeur-driven touring-style limousine wearing a hot-mama boa and carrying a lap dog. There would be placards about her in Papa Gumbo Willie McWorthy's barbershop, on the porch of Stranahan's store, and on telegraph poles all around town. Then her name would be up in a crown of bright twinkling lights above the main entrance to the Saenger Theatre which was the premier showcase in downtown Mobile in those days.

Actually by that time the way most people in Gasoline Point had begun to act whenever she came around you would have thought that she had already been away and had come back famous. Even when people were standing right next to her on the sidewalk or in a yard somewhere, it was as if they were looking at her satin smooth caramel brown skin and croquignole-frizzy hair and her diamond ring and twenty-four-carat ankle chain on stage with their eyes still glazed by the footlights.

Sometimes even when people were talking directly to her they sounded as if she were no longer a living and breathing person in the flesh anymore. It was as if to men and women alike she was a dazzlingly beautiful woman-child beyond everything else, and as such not only mysterious but also unsettling if not downright disturbing. No wonder pretty girls so often seem to be smiling, either as if in response to applause or as if in self-defense.

But Creola Calloway was never to go anywhere with any road show. It turned out that in spite of all the speculation and predictions that everybody else had been making over the years, by the time she was almost nineteen she had decided that she didn't want to leave Gasoline Point. All she wanted to do was go on having a good time, making the rounds from one jook joint and honky-tonk to the next as she had begun doing not long after she dropped out of school (truant officers or no truant officers) even before she finished the ninth grade.

Some people said that she just stayed on in Gasoline Point because she hadn't ever been able to figure out what she was supposed to do about being so good-looking except to act as if it didn't really matter. But most others realized that talk like that had more to do with bewilderment if not exasperation than with insight, because all that anybody could actually quote her as saying was that she did not want to go on the road because she did not want to leave Gasoline Point.

And that was that. She didn't even insist that what she chose to do with her own life was her own private business, because she had already made that point once and for all by dropping out of school when she did. But even so, most of the people who had always concerned themselves about her future all along went right on reacting as if her beautiful face and body were really sacred community commonwealth property and that she therefore had an inviolable obligation to turn into some sort of national credit not only to Gasoline Point and Mobile but also to the greater glory of our folks everywhere.

Nobody ever either accused her of or excused her for not having enough nerve, gall, guts, and get-up to take a chance out on the circuit and up North. Self-confidence was not the problem. Not for Creola Calloway. The problem was her lack of any interest in what, in the slogan of Mobile County Training School (and most church auxiliaries as well), was, A commitment to betterment. Given her God-given assets, that was not just disappointing and exasperating, it made her somebody even more reprehensible than a backslider. it was a betrayal of a divine trust.

That is why by the time she was twenty so many people had

given her up as a lost ball in the high weeds and no longer called
her old Creola Calloway (with a passive smile) but that old Creola
Calloway (with their eyes rolling). Nor did the outrage have
anything to do with the fact that she spent so much time hanging
out in jook joints and honky-tonks. There were many church folks
who condemned that outright to be sure, but the chances are that
if she had gone north and become a famous entertainer like, say,
Bessie Smith or Ethel Waters, she would have had their blessing
along with everybody else's.

But she stayed right on in the old Calloway house on Front
Street by the trolley line even after Miss Cute (also known as Q
for Queenie and as Q. T.), who had always been more like a very
good-looking older sister than a mother anyway, had gone up
North and decided to get married again and settle down in
Pittsburgh.

She did pay Miss Cute a visit from time to time and she also
used to take the L & N up to Cincinnati and continue on up to
Detroit to spend time with her brother every once in a while. His
name was Alvin Calloway, Jr., but everybody always called him
Brother Calloway, not as in church brother but as if you were
saying Buddy Calloway or Bubber Calloway or even Big Brother
or Little Brother Calloway. He must have been about three or four
years older than his sister and there wasn't a better automobile
mechanic in Gasoline Point before he left to go and get a job in an
automobile factory.

One time he came down for Easter in a brand-new Cadillac
and she drove back with him and was gone for ten days, and
another time she was away for a month because she also spent
some time visiting cousins in Cleveland and Chicago. Everybody
knew about those trips and also about the time she went out to
California to spend six weeks with her father, whose name was
Alvin Calloway (Senior) but who was called Cal Calloway and

who had gone out to Los Angeles not long after he came back from France with the AEF. He had a job as a carpenter in a moving picture studio.

I remember knowing that she took the southbound L & N Pan American Express from Mobile to New Orleans and changed to the Sunset Limited, which I can still see pulling out of the Canal Street Station as if with the departure bell dingdonging a piano vamp against the crash cymbal sound of the piston exhaust steam and as if with the whistle shouting California here I come like a solo above the up-tempo two-beat of the drivers driving westbound toward Texas and across the cactus country and the mountains en route to the Pacific Coast which was two whole time zones and three days and nights away.

You couldn't say that she stayed on in Gasoline Point because she hadn't even been anywhere and seen anything else. She went everywhere she wanted to go whenever she wanted to go, especially after Miss Cute left town. But she never went anywhere without a return ticket, and she always came back not only as if on a strict schedule but also almost always before most people who didn't happen to know when she left had a chance to miss her.

That was why even those who knew better used to talk as if she were always in and around town. But then she, which is to say her stunning good looks, always had been and always would be a source of confusion and anxiety. So much so sometimes that people used to accuse her of causing outbreaks of trouble that she had absolutely nothing to do with, as if she caused trouble just by being in town. As if Gasoline Point which had also come to be known and shunned as the L & N Bottoms long before Creola Calloway's parents were born had not been a hideout hammock for bayou-jettisoned African captives and runaway slaves before that and a buccaneer's hole even before that.

When she got married to Scott Henderson, whose family owned the Henderson Tailor Shop and Pressing Club, nobody expected her to settle down, and she didn't. She was going on twenty-two that summer and the whole thing was over in less than a year. Scott Henderson had left town to start his own dry cleaning business down in Miami, Florida. So when Eddie Ray Meadows, who worked in a drugstore downtown and was one of the best tap dancers around and also a pretty good shortstop and base runner, took her to the justice of the peace, people didn't give him but six months and he barely made it. Then there was Felton Edmonds from the Edmonds family of the Edmonds and McKinny Funeral Home downtown. He and his silk suits and two-tone shoes and fancy panama hats and Willys-Knight sports roadster made it through one high rolling summer.

I don't know which ones were annulled and which were divorced, but by the time she was thirty she had gotten rid of four husbands, because Willie York, better known as Memphis Willie the gambler and bootlegger who was sent to the penitentiary sometime later, was also with her for about a year.

People didn't know what to make of all of that, but they had to wag their heads and say something so the word was that she just really didn't care any more about having married than she cared about anything else, and they also decided that she didn't make things happen. She just let things happen. Not anything and everything, to be sure, just the things she became involved with. In other words, she didn't get married any of those times because she had picked out a husband for herself on her own. She just let one man like her for a while and then there would be somebody else.

One thing was always clear. She didn't have to marry or become a common-law wife to get somebody to earn a living for her. Everybody knew that as an heiress to the old Calloway place she not only had a home for herself and her own family if any for the rest of her life, but she also had Miss Sister Mattie May Billings there to run the part she rented out to long-term roomers. Everybody knew that and most people also knew that her share of the boarding house once known as River Queen Inn, which her grand-

49

father had built on Buckshaw Mill Road back during the days of William McKinley and which was being managed for her and Miss Cute by Brother Buford Larkin, came to more than enough for her to live well on, even without the old homeplace.

People used to forget about all of that when they got started on Creola Calloway, or so it seemed to me. But even so, what all the botheration always came down to was not whether she could or would earn and pay her own way as expected or would even let somebody else look out for her. No matter what folks said, everybody knew better than that. The problem was that people felt let down because she didn't do enough with herself and the extra special God-given blessing she was born with.

Not that anybody ever really expected to reap any personal profit in dollars and cents from her success. All most expected was that she would come back through town every now and then. It was not that folks had put their hopes on her coming back and changing anything around town. Others were expected to do that. All they wanted her to do was go out and become Gasoline Point's contribution to the world of show business.

Such was people's downright exasperation once they finally came to realize that they might as well give up so far as she and all of that were concerned, that the very way they called her name (behind her back to be sure) sounded as if they had already decided what to put on her headstone: CREOLA CALLOWAY—SHE COULD HAVE BEEN FAMOUS.

And yet nobody ever really hated or even disliked her. How could you not like somebody who was just as friendly as she was good-looking? She was not a nice girl because nice girls didn't ever go into the low-down joints and honky-tonks she spent so much of her time in. Still, she was such a nice person.

Yet even so, by the time I was old enough for Mama to start worrying and warning me about fooling around and getting myself all tangled up with no good full-grown women out for nothing but a good time day in and day out, it was as if Creola Calloway had become the very incarnation of all the low-down enticements that had always led so many promising schoolboys so completely astray.

That was why Little Buddy Marshall turned out to be the one who finally got to do what I too had hoped to grow up to do, if only one time, one day. When he came back from one of his L & N hobo trips and asked me if I had made any move on her yet and I told him what Mama and some others, especially Miss Minnie Ridley Stovall had been preaching for my benefit, he said, Man she may be getting on up there with a few wrinkles after all these goddamn years of fast living and all that, but man I don't care what anybody say I got to see if I can get me some of that old pretty-ass stuff.

He said, Man, I been wanting me some of old Creola ever since I found out what this goddamn thing was made for. Man, remember what we used to say when she used to say what she used to say. Man couldn't nobody else in Gasoline Point, Mobile County, Alabama, say hello sweetheart to a little mannish boy like she could, and I ain't just talking about the sound of her voice. I'm talking about couldn't nobody make it sound that good because couldn't nobody else look at you with a smile like that.

I said, Oh man. I said, You know it too. Remembering also that she was the only grown woman you didn't have to call Miss and say ma'am to. You said Creola because that is what everybody else always said and also because it was what she herself said when she wanted you to do something for her. That was when she always used to say: Hello, sweetheart. Come here sporty. Listen darling, would you like to do Creola a great big favor and run up to Stranahan's store if I say pretty please and promise you something very nice. (Oh Lord!)

What she almost always wanted was a package of Chester-field ready-rolls and two or three bottles of Coca-Cola and when you came back you knew she was always going to say, Now there's my sweetheart, and you also knew that she was always going to say, Keep the change, sporty. Then she was going to give you a hug and a kiss, and you would be that close, and she would be wearing cologne that always made her smell as good as she looked, even when she was smoking a cigarette. Some lagniappe!

But the more Little Buddy Marshall went on talking and I went on remembering, the more I wanted to change the subject because I didn't want to say anything about being on the spot, since you couldn't bring up anything about school with him anymore. You couldn't, but he could, and he did, because he already knew and he was rubbing it in without ever mentioning it.

As if I didn't know, and I also knew that he honestly felt that he, not I, was the one with the experience and nerve you needed to make a move on Creola Calloway because he, not I, was the one who had skipped city and made it back from beyond far horizons (although not yet all seven of the seas) and on his own. But I just let that go. I just said, Old Lebo, I said, Hey man, goddamn. I said, Yeah man.

To which he said, Hey man, let me tell you something for a fact. Man, I ain't never stopped having them goddamn dreams about me and old Creola. Man when I think about all the times I been thinking about that frizzly-headed quail when I was climbing up on some tough-ass northern whore, man you know I got to find out if I can handle that heifer. Man I got to see if I can make somebody that pretty whisper my name in my ear.

When I saw him again, it was about three weeks later and when he saw me he started sporty limping and whistling "Up a Lazy River," and as we slapped palms he winked and then he said, Hey man guess what? and stood straddling his left hand and snapping fingers with his right saying, Hey shit, I reckon hey shit I fucking fucking reckon.

IX

So well now, hello there, Mister College Boy, the one I had given the nod said as we came on into the upstairs room she was using that night. She was the same shade of cinnamon-bark brown as Deljean McCray, but her hair was slightly straighter and glossier and I guessed that she was about three or four years older than Deljean McCray, but her legs were not as long because she was not quite as tall as I was.

I said, Hello Miss Pretty Lady, and she smiled and said, So where you hail from handsome, and when I said, Mobile, she said, You don't tell me, and looked me up and down again, stretching her eyes as if in pleasant surprise and then she primped her mouth and said, Well go on then, Mister City Boy, you can't help it. And watched me blush.

Then she said, You know what I heard. They tell me you young sports from down around the Gulf Coast and all them cypress bayous and all that mattress moss and stuff supposed to be real hot-natured from all that salt air and fresh seafood and fresh

fruit and all them Creole spices and mixtures and fixtures and
gumbo and all them raw oysters. And I said, I don't know about all
that.

I said, I don't know anything about what other people think
about us yet because this is really my first time away from down
there, and she said, Well that's what they been telling me for don't
know how long, probably ever since I found out what it's made for.
And that's when I said what I said. Because I had been warned that
if you came across as a smart aleck you were going to find yourself
pussy-whipped and back out on the sidewalk in one short verse
and about one-half chorus if not a verse and a couple of bars.

I said, Is that supposed to be good or bad, and she said, That's
what I want to know, so come on let's find out. If I like it that means
it must be good and if I don't, it's bad. And I saw my chance and
said, Or maybe there's really nothing to it in the first place and got
myself a quick smile and the nicest squeeze I'd had since saying
goodbye to Miss Slick McGinnis.

The room surprised me. I already knew that the houses in the
district were supposed to be safer and nicer than those in Bearmash
Bottom, Gin Mill Crossing, or out on Ellis Hill Road, and that this
was the best house in the district because it catered strictly to the
campus trade. Not that I had expected any joints of any kind
anywhere in that section of Alabama to be as rowdy as just plain
old everyday back alley jook houses around Gasoline Point or
side-street joints off the waterfront in downtown Mobile. I wasn't
concerned about anything like that at all. I just hadn't expected the
room to be what it was.

I had thought that there would be just a bed and maybe two
chairs and a nightstand with a washbasin and soap and towels and
a clothes rack. But it was as if we were in one of the cozily
furnished guest rooms of a big two-story house of a prosperous
small-town businessman. Not only were there double windows
with frilly curtains, a vase of fresh flowers on the chest of drawers,

and watercolor prints and sketches of Paris, Rome, and Greece, but also a private bathroom with hot and cold running water, which was something very special everywhere except in deluxe hotels when I was a freshman.

So come on over here, sweetie pie, she said, pulling my arms around her waist and when I moved one hand up and the other down and waited, she said, Nice, very nice, you got nice manners Mobile, and when I moved my hands and waited again she said, Well all right then, sweetie pie, but just a minute, just a minute, and she stepped back and slipped off her boa-trimmed kimono and sat on the bed and kicked off her slippers and when I pulled off my shoes and stripped down, she said, Well hello sweet popper shopper. Let's have some *fun*. Let's do some *stuff*. She said, Let's have us a *ball*. She said, Me and you, baby boy, me and you, me and *you!*

You couldn't hear any voices in any of the other rooms down the hall. There was the static-blurred music and chatter on the radio downstairs for a while, but then there was only what was happening in the room where I was as she whispered sometimes with her lips and tongue touching my ear and sometimes as if to herself. But even so I was still conscious of the dark, damp mid-October night outside and the campus that far away back across town.

I had the feeling that she went on whispering not only because that was something she did sometimes but also because she really wanted me to enjoy myself. So I said, Talk to me, big mama, talk to me hot mama, talk to me pretty mama, and she said, Me and you snookie pie, me and you sweet daddy me and you sweet papa stopper, and it was a very nice ride because that was the way she wanted it to be. Because as smart about things like that as I had already become before I came to college that year, I was also sharp enough to realize that I wouldn't have been any match at all for a pro like her if she had wanted to turn me into an easy trick.

Afterward in the bathroom she said, Here, let me do this, and

I raised both arms as if she'd said hands up and she winked and
said, I hope you realize you getting some very special brown-skin
service over here schoolboy, and I said, You bet I do, Miss Stuff,
and she said, I heard that Mobile, that's pretty good Mobile if it
mean what some people mean by it, and I said, How about something you knew how to strut second to none how about something
you got to watch because it's so mellow, and she said, And what
about something you trying to hand because you already so full of
it and ain't even dry behind the ears yet.

But you still all right with me, Mobile, she said and then
she also said, You a nice boy, Mobile, I mean sure enough nice
like you been brought up to be. Don't take much to tell when it
come to something like that. When you and your buddy first
walked in down there, the very minute I laid eyes on you I said
to myself, un-hunh, un-hunh, un-hunh, and then here you come
picking me.

And I said, What did you think of that? and she said, I had
to wonder if you thought you so smart you had my number but
since there was something about you I said to myself, I'm just going
to give him the benefit of the doubt and find out what he think he
putting down. And I said, I sure am glad you did and I sure do
thank you for such a special treat, and she said, Well, that's what
you get for being such a nice boy.

While I was pulling my clothes back on, she sat on the edge
hunched forward with her legs crossed and her left elbow on her
knee smoking and asking me about Mobile and the Gulf Coast and
when she stood up I had the feeling that she really wanted us to
go on talking. So when she said, You better come back to see me
now and I really mean it, I got the feeling that she was just as
interested in talking again as she was in doing business.

I said, I sure will, but I didn't say when because I didn't have
any idea when there would be enough cash for something like that

again. There was no point in putting up a front; and you couldn't put on the poor mouth, so I just smiled and touched her as if I were really looking forward to it, and she said, You sure better.

Then she said, Come on now, I got to get you out of here so you can be back across town before that curfew sound. Ain't no use to you missing that since you already got what you come over here for, and I said, And more, much more, and she said, Tell me anything, Mobile, but you take care of yourself and hit them books and don't be no stranger over here.

Downstairs, she left me in the little sitting room to wait for my old pardner and he came in from down the hall before I even sat down, and back outside in the damp central Alabama autumn night once more with our sports jackets draped over our shoulders cape-style, we slapped palms, and I said, Hey, man, goddamn, hey, man, how can I ever thank you enough for getting Old Troop to include me on this, and he went into his penny-dreadful heh-heh-heh again and said, You can't, old pardner. It's not allowed. Absolutely not. Strictly forbidden. *Rigoureusement interdit!* which he articulated better than any student I ever met and which, what with our make-believe capes, also turned us into two elegant *flâneurs* winding our way back across fin-de-siècle Paris from Montmartre to the Left Bank.

But once we were back in Atelier 359 with the lights out but still too high to fall right off to sleep, he said, One more thing, old pardner. Tell me. When you hit the homestretch, did she start snapping her fingers, and I cut in and said, Saying sic 'em, and he said, Yes, and I said, Or maybe sic 'em baby or sic 'em daddy, and he said, So yours too, and I said, Not this one but I know what you mean and he said, It caught me by surprise but it was really something, and I said a little something idiomatic. I said, A little down-home stuff for the city boy from up north. Man, she had your number as soon as she saw us.

———

On our second visit which was during the study break just before the fall term finals and which was also a surprise treat from Old Troop, it was as if my new friend in the district had in the meantime become my old friend, if not an old long lost friend. When we checked in and turned around, she was looking down from the staircase with one hand on the railing and one on her hip.

Well, look who finally made it back, she said, talking to me but looking over my head as if at nothing in particular. Then she said, Get yourself on up here, Mobile. Where you been, boy? I thought I told you not to come making yourself no stranger over here. You make people feel like maybe you done decided not to have nothing more to do with them or something. And I said, No days like that. I said, Never no days like that for me and you.

I said, You know how it is when you're a first-term freshman, especially when you're on a full scholarship. You got to keep your grade point average up in the outstanding bracket, and you also have to convince the people on the academic merits committee that you are here because you really mean business, you see for me to make just a fair or even a good passing grade is exactly the same thing as flat flunking out.

Hey so you up here on one of them special scholarship things, she said, standing back to look me over again nodding her head up and down in what looked for all the world to me at that time with very thinly disguised fairy godmotherly pride and approval. Now that's nice. Now that really is very nice.

Then she stood back with her hands akimbo, smiling while shaking her head in mock disbelief and said, Now see there. Class. I knew it. Because I can tell. As soon as I set eyes on you, I said to myself, um-hunh, um-hunh, um-hunh, and I also said, I bet he think he cute too, but you didn't smile that kind of smile and that's how come I liked you right off. You know what you smile like with them bright eyes squinting like that? A very nice boy full of mischievousness.

But talking about some more smart eyes, don't think I didn't pick up on how that cute buddy you come over here with was casing this joint right along with all them friendly smiles and respectful manners Sarajean was telling me about him and she said he is definitely the nicest northern city boy she ever come across and she been in this life for a whole lot of more years than I been. Some we get in here think they so much because they from up there, and don't know doodly squat. But she say your buddy got real class and she swear he also just thumbs down the smartest fellow she ever met anywhere.

She sure did get that right, I said, and she said, I told her ain't no flies on my down-home Mobile boy either. Then reaching for my belt buckle she said, But later for all that. Now come on, show me how much you been missing me because it's been so long.

It was the same room as before. There was the same blurred-static sound of radio music and chatter somewhere downstairs again, but as she helped me out of my shorts and I sat down to pull off my socks this time there was also the dry smokeless warmth from the flame-yellow grill of the gas space heater because the temperature outside was dropping toward the freezing point.

Then as she began whispering and brushing her warm gingerbread-spongy lips against my neck and ears again as before, but also with a few new words added, there was also the shushing and shivery winter night breeze buffeting the shuttered and shuddering window frames and whining and shrilling away through the December bareness of the yard trees. But after a very little while all of that was only another part of what I would remember as the background for me and her doing me and you and you and me the second time.

So if I ask you who she was you going to tell me? she said, pulling on her kimono and following me into the bathroom again, and when I said, Who *who* was, she said, Now come on boy. Don't be trying to crosstalk me.

She said, Now, you know good and well what I'm talking about and don't come telling me I don't know what I'm talking about. The one you learned all of your nice little bedroom manners from; that's who. You might be one of them scholarship geniuses that can learn anything in a split second. But you can't fool me about nothing like this, boy. You didn't just pick up on something on no one go-round. Some woman know exactly what she doing had a hold of you and don't tell me she didn't.

She sure did, I said, *thinking about Miss Slick McGinnis and her velvet smooth tea-cake tan skin and her Josephine Baker rubber-doll body, and how when she used to come click clacking along Buckshaw sidewalk past Papa Gumbo Willie McWorthy's barbershop and up the steps and into Stranahan's store all the men and boys on the block used to fall silent and then just look at each other and shake their heads and also about how the windup gramophone record that went with the way she walked was the one with the words that said, I want to go where you go and do what you do then I'll be happy.*

But I didn't name any names because that was not what was expected. All you had to do was admit that there was somebody. So I just said that there was somebody who decided that was the way she was going to help keep me out of trouble and finish high school and win my chance to go to college as so many people by that time had come to expect me to do.

Well, good for her, she said, and as we came back into the bedroom you could also hear the wind rising and whirring through the bare branches outside the shutters again. She all right with me whoever she is and wherever she may be these days, she said, waiting for me to put everything back on. I hope you know how lucky you been and I am pretty sure you do and that's another reason you all right with me with your little old cute, sly fox, narrow-eye smile.

Then as she hooked her arm into mine and we came on along the hall to the head of the stairs, she also said, I know you know good and, well, I ain't just talking about controlling your nature because I'm satisfied I don't have to tell you ain't nobody going to be complaining about no wham-bam-thank-you-ma'am in no house like this. Now if I was to be talking about some tough-ass old hens want you spend all night with them, that's another thing.

She said, When it come to all of that what I mean is, you might know how to do what you supposed to do with that nice sweet thing all night, but the first thing you better know is when you supposed to keep it in your pants. So the one that schooled you about that deserve a lot of credit, she said.

And then she said, What I'm trying to tell you right now, that you all right with me because whoever she was she didn't spoil you so rotten that you go around acting like somebody supposed to feel like you doing them a big favor just because you having something to do with them. I'm just trying to tell you how much a woman can appreciate you for being so nice on top of all that other stuff. So now just get on out of here and I hope I see you again before long.

I didn't realize that all of that had anything to do with her in any sense that was directly personal and private until she told me what she told me about herself that next time, which was also the Old Trooper's last treat and so also the end of the orientation leeway he had allowed his two trail recruits to get themselves zeroed in on campus and in certain outlying regions as well.

So what I remember thinking about as we whistled our way through town and then came on across the highway and into the district that night was about how in the letter with my roommate's February allowance (and the treat), the Old Trooper had used the word triangulation, not orientation. Both were about map making and map reading and also about personal adjustment, but triangulation was also a military term that was very much about target practice.

That was what was on my mind when I rearrived in the district on my third visit that Thursday night. It was not as if I didn't also remember everything that had been said the time before. After all, I had repeated it verbatim to my roommate the following morning. But one reason that I hadn't stopped to think much less to consider about any of it was that by that time I had become so used to having people talk to me about such things that most of it usually sounded like reiteration rather than information.

Not that I ever really closed my ears to any of it. Not me. Not Miss Melba's Scooter. Not Miss Tee's Mister. Because for all the clichés, platitudes, and sometimes downright mushy sentimentality about making folks proud (mostly without any mention whatsoever of envy, resentment, backbiting, spite, or slander) and for all the same old stuff about taking advantage of opportunities other people either never had or had and didn't take, there was still the fact that whatever they said was something they sincerely believed they were obliged to say so perhaps the main point of it all was to remind you of precisely that which everybody knew you were supposed to be mindful of already.

Anyway, it was not until she said what she said while I was getting dressed that third time that I realized that she was really concerned about something that had much more to do with her own personal situation in particular than with me on general principle.

She had asked me to tell her some more about growing up on the outskirts of Mobile, and when I came to the part about school and told her about how a lot of students used to come all the way out to Mobile County Training School not only from within the city limits of downtown Mobile itself and from Prichard and Cedar Grove and Chickasaw Whistler and Maysville, but also from as far away across the bay as Daphne, Fairhope, and Magnolia Springs, she said, Now see there, you never learn unless you ask. Boy, that sounds just like the kind of school I'm sure going to be trying my best to get my Roger in one of these days when he old enough.

Roger was a three-year-old son that she had left with her mother, who was now living in Fort Deposit. She didn't even mention anything at all about who Roger's father was, and I didn't ask anything. From what she said about how she ran away from home to go to Birmingham, I was pretty sure that she had not been married and that when she became pregnant she had had to look out for herself, but she mentioned that only in passing because what she was mainly if not only really interested in telling me about was the kind of man she wanted Roger to be.

Not *what* she wanted him to be, such as a doctor, lawyer, businessman, teacher, or a political leader. That was going to be up to him to choose once he had come along far enough in school to make his own choice. The main thing she wanted him to become was somebody worthwhile and also somebody you could always count on.

I just want him to have his chance to make something out of hisself. I sure God don't want him to end up on on chain gang in no penitentiary. I don't want him out there trying to lie and steal and cheat and double-cross his way. Just look at you, she said. That's what I'm talking about. Done made it all the way up here in college because you can make it on your own scholarship. That's what I'm talking about. I'm talking about, I want my Roger to turn out like you turning out so far. Boy, your folks got to be mighty proud of you and I'm sure you know it too, you rascal you.

X

A s for mothers, I said one night not long afterward, I have three at the same time. Because along with Mama herself there had always been Miss Tee, and then when I had come that far as a pupil over at Mobile County Training School there was also Miss Lexine Metcalf who not only said but also acted as if I also belonged to her.

The only thing I remember that Mama actually told me about my kinship to her was about how all babies came from the soft dark insides of a very special stump hole deep in the brambles and moss-fringed thickets where the baby man hid you like a seed to be found like an Easter egg on your birthday by the woman he picked to be your mother, who was the one who swaddled you to her bosom and gave you nourishment and kept you safe from the bad old booger man. Which was why your mother was the one you already owed your obedience long before you came to realize that you also had a father.

That was all she had ever told me before I overheard what

she said that night at Mister Ike Meadow's wake, and that is the
way she let it stay even when she told me what she told me about
not letting that thing in my pants get me in trouble because she had
decided that the time had come when she had to start warning me
about getting girls in the family way. As for the contradiction
between this version of the miracle of birth and the other, I am
pretty sure that she just took it for granted that by that time I had
found out enough about men and women to understand exactly
what she was concerned about and the main point of it was to keep
me from having to drop out of school to get married. In any case,
she never revised her original version of the arrival of babies, just
as she never revised her original version of Santa Claus.

All I had ever heard about me and Miss Tee was that she was
my auntie, and at first that was what I used to call her. Actually,
what I used to say was Ann Tee. Then I changed it to Miss Tee.
But what she called me was not her nephew but her Mister as in
Mister Man, and I always knew that she was a very special kind
of auntie, because everybody knew that she was not Mama's flesh
and blood sister, like Aunt Sue from Atmore and Aunt Sis from
Greenville. In fact, she almost always acted as if Mama and Papa
were really *her* aunt and uncle.

For the most part, people in Gasoline Point in those days
didn't spend very much time puzzling over such relationships
unless there was some special reason to do so. After all, just about
everybody in town had aunts and uncles, not to mention cousins
close and distant who included perhaps as many if not more
self-elected kinfolks as blood relatives. But there were also always
at least a few aunts- and uncles-at-large around. Like Aunt Classie
Belsaw, for instance, and Uncle Jim Bob Ewing, to name only two,
who for their part called everybody not Nephew or Niece but
either Son or Daughter or Brother or Sister, meaning little brother
and little sister.

I don't remember ever hearing anybody wondering about

what all of that was about and certainly not about how it all came about. It was just the way things were and one day you realized that you already knew about it. In due time, you also came to realize that there were also aunts- and uncles-at-large who were called Mama and Papa and Daddy or even Papadaddy, as in Big Mama and Big Daddy and once again it was as if nobody had ever had to stop and define them because somehow you had already found out that old folks were who they were by virtue of being survivors-in-residence, who were there to tell the tale, who could give eyewitness testimony about bygone but ever-to-be-remembered times in which definitive events came to pass.

Nor did anyone have to question the fact that such mamas (and hot mamas) as Ma Rainey the blues singer and vaudeville prima donna and such papas and daddies as even Papa Gumbo Willie McWorthy were neither older nor wiser than such venerable aunts- and uncles-at-large as Aunt Classie Belsaw and Uncle Jim Bob Ewing who after all were the very embodiment of endurance and wisdom. Hot mamas and papadaddies were who they were because they were not only experts in their line of work but also pros and past masters who were qualified by the unique richness of personal experience to exemplify for peers and juniors alike how things should be done. Thus, when a young man called himself Papa or Daddy, he was bragging that he was so much better than his competitors that he could turn any contest into a demonstration lesson in fundamentals.

What made such youthful presumption acceptable to people in Gasoline Point in those days was the fact that it showed that you were not afraid to put yourself on the spot. If it turned out that you were only running off at the mouth and couldn't perform on the level you had set up for yourself, you only brought public disgrace on yourself. Once you proved yourself, you could admit that you were the champion who must defend his title. That was okay. But

any further expression of gratuitous self-esteem was soundly condemned as the height of unforgivable arrogance.

Miss Tee was the expert auntie who told me about fairy-tale
beanstalks, and she also used to used to say Jack be nimble, Jack
be quick, Jack jump over the candlestick, coping me up and out
and dedoodling me over and back down and enfolding me to the
bosom of herself again. She also riddled me riddles and nourished
me on nursery rhymes and caught me with catches and girded me
for existential guessing games.

She had a good-fairy smile and fairy-godmother ring fingers,
and I can still remember her story-time voice saying once upon a
time over my shoulder and that close to my ear as she rocked me
rock-a-bye in Mama's rocking chair. It was as if all of that had
always been there along with everything else, and even before I
was old enough to know what a storybook as such actually was, I
could help her turn the page so that I could look at the pictures
on the next page while her voice went on spinning out the yarn of
the story for that day.

As far back as I can recollect, seeing her coming back again
I can also remember that it was as if she had only just rearrived
from the far blue ever-and-ever land of storybook castles and boy
blue derring-do once more and that I was going to find out something else about how heroes set forth to seek their fortune and
about how they prepare themselves to brave the elements and to
slay dragons and giants and other dangerous creatures because
such, being their destiny, was also their duty.

I was still very young when she got married to Mister Paul
Miles Boykin, a stacking-yard straw boss at Buckshaw Mill, but
from then on I knew what neighborhood she lived in, because you
could see her house from Miss Betty Dubose's corner when on

your way up Dodge Mill Road toward the crawfish pond and the streetcar loop; and you could also see it from the end of Gins Alley as soon as you passed Miss Blue Eula's gate on your way to the L & N post office and looked to your left along the street that ran from the tank yard and across Dodge Mill Road to the A T & N and the pecan orchard.

Whichever route you took, her house was only about two and a half blocks away and so was still a part of Gasoline Point although it was also another neighborhood, just as Gins Alley was still another neighborhood. It was called Main Street, but it really should have been called Second Street because the main thoroughfare where all of the business concerns were located and along which most of the traffic came and went was Buckshaw Road, which later on (at the time when the Cochrane Bridge was built across that part of Mobile River) became a part of U.S. 90 and the old Spanish Trail.

When you opened the gate there was a cowbell sound, and there were flower beds on both sides of the brick walk as you came on toward the trellis screening the swing porch. Then when you came up the steps by the potted plants and into the parlor there were heavy draperies that matched the chair cushions and a big bouquet of fresh flowers in a blue vase on the lace-covered center table in front of the settee and bright blue-and-yellow flower patterns on the store-bought wallpaper.

I also remember the high beds with the fancy fringed counterpanes and frilly window curtains I saw as we went through the back rooms on our way to the kitchen that first time, and after we ate a sandwich Miss Tee and Mama went on talking and drinking coffee. She said I could go out into the backyard if I wanted to, and as soon as I opened the door onto the screened-in porch, I saw the toy store playthings.

Then that house turned out to be the first place I was allowed to go when I became old enough to be that far from the chinaberry yard on my own, and in the beginning you had to go by way of Gins Alley because of all the heavy traffic along Dodge Mill Road, and when you arrived she was always waiting either at the gate or on the front steps, and there was always something that she said she had been saving as a little surprise, and when time was up she always went with you to the gate and handed you a package to take back to Mama.

The best times were when Mister Paul Miles Boykin was not there. Because whenever he was, even if he just happened to make a quick circle by the house during the twelve o'clock whistle break, he would be watching and cutting his eyes at you even when he didn't say the same old thing about not being able to waste all of his time playing when he was a child.

One time he showed up at our house as if from the clear blue sky (but probably directly from a spluttering argument with Miss Tee) and asked Mama if he could hire me to run errands and do chores for him on a weekly basis so I could realize that I had to earn my keep and pay my way because nothing comes free in this world. And Mama said, Be time enough for him to realize that, and she said, He got to be a child before he can be a man, and she also said, He sure better mind his manners and show due respect for grown folks because God knows I don't mind their chastising him and I better not hear tell of him opening his mouth back at them neither, let alone sassing them. But me and Whit the ones raising him and I don't want nobody bossing him around and abusing him for no little old few cents a week, don't care who it is, and don't care what color neither. To which he said, I'm Edie's husband now and I'm thinking of his welfare, and Mama said, I want him to grow up a step at a time, and he sure will be coming to all of that soon enough. Too soon if you ask me.

———

Then one day Deljean McCray was there standing on the front steps below Miss Tee waiting for me as I came through the cowbell gate. She was that much older and that many more inches taller than I was and she stood with her arms akimbo, smiling down at me like a newfound cousin. Then she took my hand and we went around the house to the backyard, and the first thing we ever played on was the seesaw, and I still get a sweet, warm feeling every time I remember how she looked bouncing and kicking her heels and opening her long rubbery cinnamon-brown legs with her skirt billowing and shutting like a parasol as she sang, Seesaw, cut the butter, seesaw. Then we also had a good time with the toy store playthings on the screened-in kitchen porch, and when I came back outside to the live oak and got on the swing, she stood up behind me and pumped so high that you could see out over the back fence and all the way across the dog-fennel meadow between there and the telegraph poles above the mill-quarter's houses along that part of Buckshaw Road.

She said, So you the little old cute Scooter boy Miss Edie Belle always carrying on so much about be coming over here, and she held my hand again, looking at me with her head tilted and her eyes twinkling with catlike curiosity and puppylike mischief. Then she said, Boy, Miss Edie Belle sure real crazy about you, always calling you her little Mister. Just wait till you see my little Mister. He'll be coming over for a visit. So this is you, she said, and then she said, and I guess you all right with me, too. So you want to be friends and play-like cousins.

I said okay because I was already very glad that she was going to be there. I said, You all right with me, too, Deljean. Because I liked her cinnamon-brown skin and the cinnamon-brown tree bark she chewed and smelled like even when she also smelled somewhat like sardine oil, and I also liked the Vaseline sheen on her braids although I never did like girls with braided hair as much as I liked frizzly-headed girls like Charlene Wingate. In those days

I liked it better when girls with hair like that wore it either bobbed and poroed like Miss Slick McGinnis or hot-combed and styled like the most popular blues singers and vaudeville entertainers, and so did she as I found out as soon as she was old enough for it to be dressed for special occasions.

When I went back over there that next time, I could tell that she was glad to see me even before she said what she said, and I said I was very glad to see her too, and she said, Now come on now tell the truth now you're not just playing with me because you come over here to see Miss Edie Belle. I'm talking about sure enough now, Scooter, saying my name exactly as somebody does who has been thinking about you since you were there the last time, and I said, Me too, Deljean. I said, I'm talking about sure enough too. And she said, Well, I reckon we must still be good friends then so come on, let's go play.

The time after that was when she said, Maybe if you ask your mama maybe Miss Edie Belle will let me come over to your house sometime and play too, and I said I would and I did and that was when I realized that she hadn't met anybody else her size to play with yet because Mister Paul Miles Boykin did not want her to get herself led astray by a pack of good-for-nothing mill-quarters niggers. Not that I was really surprised one bit. So I certainly was not surprised when she told me that as soon as he found out that she and I were becoming playmates, he said what he said about her not having any time to be working loafing around playing with the likes of little old mister precious me instead of earning her bed and board.

It was not long afterward that she ran away the first time. She was gone for a week and I missed her as if I had known her all my life. I missed her every day not because I had ever seen her every day but because I didn't know where she was or if I would ever see her again, and when Mama told me she was back, I could hardly wait to see her again and when I got there she saw me coming through the gate and said, Here come Scooter, and she was still trying to smile down at me even with her face bruised and swollen like it was because Mister Paul Miles Boykin had finally traced and found her up in Chickasaw Bend. He had slapped and cuffed her all the way back along the A T & N railroad in the dark.

That's all right. Don't you worry about me, Scooter, she said when I touched her and asked her if it still hurt bad, and she didn't cry when she told about what had happened.

In fact, I don't remember ever seeing her cry about anything. Sometimes she used to get so mad about something that her eyes would water but that was not the same thing as crying because when you cry about something happening to you that means you feel sorry for yourself. But when you get so angry about something that tears almost come that just shows how much determination you have.

She says, Boy you don't know, Scooter. Boy, you don't know nothing at all about my uncle Paul Miles Boykin. She said, Boy you ain't never seen nobody like that in your whole life. She said, I'm talking about every time he think he got to chastise somebody about something, here he come, slapping you up side the head before he even tell you what he mad about, and when you try to move out of the way and ask him what's wrong, he subject to pick up anything he can get his hands on and chuck it at you. And then come talking about he love me because I'm his flesh and blood kin and he don't want me to end up in the gutter and some old stuff like that, I declare, Scooter.

But that's all right with me, Scooter. She also said, That's all right with me because I don't care no more because I know good and well he crazy. I declare before God that man just as angry as he can be. And you know something? If it wasn't for Miss Edie Belle I never would be coming back here no more. Don't care if he tried to kill me to make me come back. He the one always talking about looking after me because I'm his dead sister's child, but Miss Edie Belle she the one know how to be somebody's auntie and treat you like you supposed to do what you do around the house because you at *home* and you got your tasks just like everybody else. But him, I'm telling you Scooter. Boy, you pretty lucky. I know what I'm talking about. You got Miss Melba and Uncle Whit and you got Miss Edie Belle on top of that, and they all treat you like you somebody special, she said, and you know why, and I said, Why? and she said, Because they want you to be somebody special and you know something, me too.

I don't remember how old I was when Miss Tee first said you are my mister because it is as if that is what she had always called me, and I cannot remember when I didn't already remember her voice and her eyes with her face that close and then her cheeks against mine and her godmotherly arms around my shoulders smelling like rainbows look.

But however young I may still have been at the time in question, I was also already old enough to have heard enough of her storybook stories to realize that when she put the tips of her fingers on your shoulders and held you an arm's length away smiling her fairy godmother smile at you, it was her secret way of saying arise Sir Knight and sally forth doing good deeds time after time after time in place after place after place.

So first there was Mama herself, whose little scootabout manchild I already was even before I was yet old enough to stay up late enough to hear the tales told on midwinter nights in the semicircle around the fireplace and during midsummer evenings on the swing porch with mosquito smoke rising and spreading in the chinaberry yard. Then there was also Miss Tee who began calling me her Mister in her storybook voice rocking me back and forth in Mama's cane-bottom rock-a-bye riverboat rocking chair.

By the time Little Buddy Marshall came along, I had outgrown most of the playthings in Miss Tee's backyard and what he and I used to spend most of our times together doing was rambling here and there and elsewhere like explorers and pioneers who were bred and born in the briar patch and we also hunted with a slingshot and the main game we lived to play was baseball. Sometimes I also thought of myself as a boxer with eyes and hands as quick as Joe Gans and a six-inch uppercut like the one and only Jack Johnson.

When he stopped in with me to meet her the first time that day when we were on our way to the shortcut through the kite pasture to get to the foot of Buckshaw Mill Road and the construction camp at the site where the Cochrane Bridge was going to be built, I knew he would like her and the first chance he got he nudged me and whispered, Hey shit I reckon old buddy boy, hey shit I reckon. Then when the time finally came to open her surprise package of sandwiches and tea cake cookies that we had promised to save until the twelve o'clock whistles started, he also said, Man, you sure got yourself some big auntie.

And that is when he also said, Now that's what I call a sure enough fairy story godmother, buddy boy, which was really something coming from him, because as much as he always liked all of the things you found out about from the chimney corner and the steps of the swing porch and especially from the barbershop, he really didn't have very much interest in storybooks as such. As far as he was concerned, there was no difference between storybooks and schoolbooks, and he never did come to like anything at all about going to school, not even the playground activities. He didn't even like football and basketball and volleyball, which were all school-term games in those days. Later on when cowboy movies began to become popular, he liked the adventures of William S. Hart and Tom Mix and Buck Jones and Ken Maynard and hated crooks like Bull Montana as much as I did, but he never did become interested in reading anything about the wild West either, not even the Indians.

But whether Little Buddy Marshall knew it or not, Miss Tee was not only what fairy godmothers were really about, she had also always been a part of what school bell time was all about and when I became school age, she had been the one who gave me my first book satchel and blackboard eraser and collapsible aluminum drinking cup, and Mama had let her be the one to take me to be registered in the primer class at Mobile County Training School that first Monday morning.

XI

You couldn't see any part of the downtown business district from anywhere on the campus, and except during the wee hours and on weekends you couldn't even hear the courthouse clock striking until you rounded the curve and passed by the wrought-iron gate to the old plantation mansion known as the Old Strickland Place. But you could walk all the way from the academic area to Old Confederate Square in less than twenty minutes.

Then you were at the hub of a cotton market town that was also the county seat, and across North Main Street from the sheriff's office and the jail and the municipal complex was the Farmer's Enterprise Bank and from that corner you could see along the sidewalk past the movie theater and the next street to the brick and lumber yard of the Carmichael Construction Supply Company and you could also see all of the stores on the other three sides of the elm-shaded square.

In those days there was also a Merchants Bank, and there

were also two drugstores, a Woolworth's, a Bradley's Furniture, and I don't know exactly how many clothing stores, specialty shops, cafes, and lunch counters, but I do remember how Goldwyn's Dry Goods store and Ransom's Bargain Emporium used to look, and everybody remembers Tate and Davidson's two-story department store.

My old roommate has a pretty good reason to remember the young women's Intercollegiate Toggery shop that was next door to Tate and Davidson's in those days, but most people have probably long since forgotten Dudley Philpot and his General Merchandise Store. Sometimes I forget all about him, too. I wonder if Will Spradley has ever forgotten, but I'm pretty certain that you would have to prod Giles Cunningham for a while and then he could probably say, Yeah, I think I can picture the old son-of-a-bitch. What the hell happened and what the hell was it all about?

The heavy interstate traffic westbound toward Montgomery and points south to Florida and the Gulf Coast and eastbound toward Phoenix City and the Georgia state line, Atlanta, and points north, came through on the south side of the square, so from the corner where the telephone central was you could see gas stations and automobile dealers' pennants in both directions and the bus stop beyond the light and power building.

The downtown post office was one block due south of the square on the tree-lined street which was called South Main and also South End and which was also where the white supremacist white high school, several white Protestant churches, and the neatly kept but not very old homes of a number of the most prosperous local white businessmen lived in those days.

Most of the downtown white families who could trace their bloodlines back to the earliest settlers lived on North Main, also known as North End which was an avenue of mostly pre–Civil War homes and with a center strip of shrubbery and flower beds and which began on the north side of the square and ended two blocks beyond the corner where it turned into a thoroughfare leading out to the campus.

As I had already found out in the library during the week before I graduated from Mobile County Training School, what the earliest settlers had originally established back during the days even before Alabama became a colony was a French trading post on an old Creek Indian trail. Then the post had become an English crossroads settlement and after that a federal garrison during the time of the Andrew Jackson anti-Indian campaign that ended with the Battle of Horseshoe Bend. It had become a cotton market town and the county seat during the flush times before the Civil War, none of which ever gave it any claim to fame even in Alabama. But since the turn of the century, it had been known all over the country as a college town.

What you saw as the bus pulled in were the mud-caked, dust-powdered jalopies and trucks and also a few horse-drawn buckboard wagons parked diagonally into the curb around the square, and there were the late summer shade trees and the concrete park benches along the gravel walks, and the gray stone Civil War monument to honor the brave.

It was the statue of a Confederate army infantryman facing North Main, and around the pedestal there was a spiked wrought-iron fence enclosing a flower bed in which, as I found out later on, there were always flowers in bloom, even in the dead of winter when they had to be grown in terra-cotta pots in a greenhouse and transferred pot by pot and embedded in straw and pine needles.

So I knew that I would also find out that you-know-which townspeople would have, if not one thousand plus one or more tall tales, riddles, rhymes, catches, and jokes to retell about Old Man Johnny Reb, as they called the rifleman, they would have at least two or three dozen. All you had to do was listen. You didn't even have to be alert. All you had to do was be in the right place at the right time.

And to be sure, there was one that you could always count on hearing repeated or, indeed, replayed every year when the first really hard cold snap hit town. All you had to do was be someplace, say like the old Greyhound bus station when the lie swapping used to get started in the semicircle of hand and rump warmers huddled around the radiator in the waiting room, as if it were an old potbelly stove.

Man, talking about a cold day. Man, Old man Johnny Reb up yonder on the courthouse square feel this weather this morning. Man, I bet you anything old stuff got his boney butt ass down off that goddamn thing last night.

Man, I don't blame him a bit.

Got rid of that old musket and brought his frostbitten peckerwood ass on down off from up there in a hurry, pardner.

Man, when old hawk hit that sapsucker, he said time to unass this area, colonel sir.

Man, so that's who that was I seen all snuggled up over yonder on the sidewalk by the drugstore last night.

Man, doing what?

Man, what you reckon? Asking somebody where he can get him a long pull-on, a fifth of sour mash, white lightning, rotgut, or anything with some kick to it.

Now, man, you know Old Man Johnny Reb know better than that. So what did you tell him?

Man, I told him that even a short snort been against the law in this county ever since they passed that Eighteenth Amendment back in nineteen-nineteen.

Man, you told him right. Been right up there with the county jail less than a block off to his right elbow all this time now.

But shoot, y'all. Maybe that's exactly how come he know good and well

*you can get all the bootleg liquor you can pay for right here in the city limits,
Prohibition or no Prohibition. All you got to do is make the right contact,
and you look just like a drinking man to me.*

*Yeah, man, but Old Man Johnny Reb suppose to be up there watching
out for the Yankees.*

*Yeah, but, man, maybe the Yankees Old Man Johnny really on the
lookout for is them revenue agents. Man, I wouldn't put it pass Cat Rogers.
Man, peckerwoods hate them folks.*

*Man, I don't care what Old Man Johnny Reb supposed to be doing
up there, his gray ass liked to froze blue and dropped off last night.*

There were also mud-caked and dust-powdered jalopies and
trucks and more buckboards all along the side streets where the
markets, the grocery stores, and the hardware and repair shops
were in those days. But most of the larger trucks and flatbed trailers
were always pulled up on the back streets and in the alleys off the
back streets where the loading ramps of the seed, feed, and fertilizer warehouses were.

I used to stay away from these blocks, especially on Saturdays, because I didn't want to have to see all of the crap games so
many of the farmhands always used to seem to make the weekly
trip into town to get into with the local hustlers. Not that I was
against gambling as such on any principle. Certainly not on any
principle based on the conventional morality underlying the disapproval of the church folks of Gasoline Point.

Not me. Not the self-elected godson of the likes of old
Luzana Cholly and Stagolee Dupas *(fils)* plus Gus the Gator all
rolled in one. Not the longtime scoot buddy of Little Buddy
Marshall. Not the one to whom the sight of sailors and longshore-
men rolling dice in the cargo sheds along the piers off Commerce
Street and elsewhere on the waterfront was as much a part of the
storybook world of the seven seas as the dry-dock elevators and

the foghorns and the acres of naval stores out at Taylor Lowenstein's maritime supply yards.

But I felt the way I felt about the back street crapshooters because it was as if they were still stuck in the same rut as the slaves of a hundred years ago, who used to be brought into town by the plantation master or overseer to reload the cotton wagons with supplies and provisions, and then used to spend their free time gambling away whatever slaves had to bet and fight each other about while the master or overseer finished his transactions and no doubt also found amusement elsewhere.

Not all slaves spent their precious free time in town on Saturday, shooting craps and indulging in frivolity, to be sure. According to many of the most often repeated storybook as well as fireside yarns, there were also those would-be and soon-to-be north-bound fugitives who deliberately gave off an air of frivolity not to spend such precious free time to pay court to in-town house servants if not sweethearts brought in on wagons from other plantations, but to make contact with whoever (sometimes male, sometimes female) could pass on the latest news and practical operational grapevine information concerning the signs, signals, passwords, and timetables of the local trunk line of the Underground Railroad.

Surely some instances of runaway slaves using the dice game as a cover have been recorded as historical fact. But in the stories I grew up hearing, the very notion of an invisible network of black and white people working together to help slaves steal away to freedom was no less farfetched to the overwhelming majority of back alley bone-rollers as all of the preaching and praying and singing about chariots taking you to heaven somewhere in the sky, and they almost always poked fun at it one way or another. Some said and may actually have convinced themselves that the so-called Underground Railroad was either a trick that Old Master and the overseer played to find out who they could trust, or it was a trap set up by rogue peckerwoods who stole slaves from one plantation and sold them to another in another place.

Anyway I was scandalized, outraged, and all but exasperated as soon as I turned the corner and saw them and realized what they were doing that bright blue second Saturday afternoon of that first October. There they were and I was already that close and there was nothing you could do about it except try to get on along past it as if I didn't even see them. But one of them had already spotted me the minute I came in sight.

Well, goddamn, if here ain't another one of them.

What they doing coming all around back up in here? Ain't nobody sent for none of them as I knows of.

Me neither. Maybe he lost or something.

I wouldn't be a bit surprised once you get their head out of all them books.

Hey, you lost Mister Collegeboy? Hey, you, yeah, you. I'm talking to you. Yeah you. I axed you a question. You want something around here, Mister Collegeboy? What you looking for around here? What you looking at? Ain't you never seen nobody rolling no bones before? Ain't you never seen nobody drinking no whiskey before? Well, now you can tell them you seen some low-down niggers galloping the shit out of them old affikan dominoes all over the place back in here and looka here, you can also tell them you seen me drinking myself some good old corn whiskey and then tell them I say win, lose, or draw I'm still going to have enough left to buy me some good old cookshop grub and then I going to buy me some good old city girl pussy. You goddamn right, I going buy me some county seat whorehouse pussy.

Aw, man, a not so loudmouthed one said, them college boys don't even know what you talking about. Them college boys studying about bookkeeping and joggerfy and all them kind of things. Them college boys ain't got no time to be fooling around with what you talking about.

Now wait a minute, another one said. That ain't the way I heard it. Now the way I heard it, them books ain't the only thing them college boys like to stick their nose up in, if you get my latter clause.

Hey, wait a minute there, the loud one said again, coming toward me for the first time as I moved on along the block. I had slowed down just because I knew they had expected me to speed up. Hey, hold on there boy when I'm talking to you.

That's when I stopped and turned and said what I said, which had exactly the effect I had wanted and expected it to have.

I said, Sounds to me like somebody is just about to let his big loud snaggle mouth get his bony ass kicked raw, and he stopped where he was and then he said, Who you think you talking to and I said, Ain't nothing to think about, old pardner. I'm talking to anybody too square to know that when the son-of-a-bitch he woofing at get through stomping his ass, he won't even want to *hear* about no pussy for a month of Saturdays. I said, If you looking for somebody to cut you a new asshole, I'm just the son-of-a-bitch to oblige you.

That was when he seemed to decide that moral outrage was the better part of valor. Hey, y'all hear this, y'all heard him, supposed to be some kind of high-class college boy and listen what kind of language he using—you ain't no better than anybody else. But he had turned and was talking to them, not me.

That was when he suddenly had to realize that he had no way of knowing anything at all about me, and my guess is that he didn't really know anything about any other college boys either. So that's when he said, See there, and then said, So that's a Mister Collegeboy for you. Suppose to be up there getting all that high-class education and just listen at him. Y'all heard him. You can't even make a little joke without here he coming talking all that old gutter language and still think somebody supposed to *respect* them.

But he was talking *about* me. Not *to* me. To *them*. To everybody present *except* me. He didn't even *look* in my direction again. Obviously he was somehow totally oblivious to the likes of Daddy Shakehouse Anderson, also known as the Nighthawk or Big Shit Pendleton from Galveston, Texas, or Speckle Red, also known as Florida Red, the Juice Head, or Sneaky Pete Davis, the First Lord of the Outlying Regions and a few other certified campus thugs that I had already met even then. Not to mention my own roommate.

XII

What finally happened to Little Buddy Marshall when I was in the eleventh grade was the end of something that had already been underway for some time even before he began to talk about it the way he kept on doing throughout the whole summer of the year before. Sooner or later he would bring everything we talked about back around to that, and when I said what I said about school I knew exactly what he was going to say again.

He said, Man, like I been telling you all this time, man you welcome to Old Lady Metcalf and all that old hickory butt roll-call and blackboard do-do, and them dripping goddamn ink pens and them goddamn checker-back composition tablets. Man, every time I think about all them old stop and go examination periods, and man don't mention them report cards, and you got to take them home and get them signed!

He said, Man you all right with me, Scooter. You know that, but man, hey shit, I reckon I got to be hauling ass to hell on out of this old Mobile, Aladambama, and all this little old two-by-four stuff around these parts. Man, I got to go somewhere else. Man, I got to hit the goddamn road. Man, that's all I can think about.

He said, Man, you know good and well you always been all right with me, starting right off from the get-go at the pump shed. I know you know that, Scooter. Everybody around here know that. But, man, when it comes to them old henhouse teachers over there on the hill ringing them goddamn bells and flopping them shit-ass foot rulers and watching everybody like a goddamn hawk, I am sorry, man. You can put up with all that kind of stuff because you like books, Scooter, and all them other old games and stuff and that's you. But me, man, I don't give a goddamn shit about any of that old shit and that's me. So that's you and that's me, and I'm just saying I got to get myself on out of here and see me some of the real sure enough world for my own damn self.

Then he said, Any day now Scooter you just wait and see, and I knew better than to try to talk him out of anything once he had said what he had said the way he had said it, because what he had decided was that he was going to take a big risk on something come what may, and practical advice didn't mean anything to him anymore. So I just said, Boy, which way you heading, man? And he said, Shoot, I'm just going, man (because he knew that I knew that his departure heading was going to be due north and then maybe northeast), and when I find me a place I like I might stay there for a while and then move on until I come to somewhere else.

I said, Sheeoot man. I said, Goddamn. I said, I already miss you too much as it is, Lebo. Because ever since I had become an Early Bird I was also almost always busy doing special extracurricular projects not only for Miss Lexine Metcalf but also Miss Edna Teale Wilcox, who is the one I always remember whenever I hear "High Society" because that was one of the piano numbers she used to play as march-in music after the flag-raising ceremony, and who was also Mister B. Franklin Fisher's assembly program coordinator and was also going to be my advanced French teacher and also my college preparatory counselor when I reached the twelfth grade.

There was also the fact that as soon as you achieved the status of a top-perching Early Bird, your name was added to the principal's senior high school campus duty roster, which rotated weekly assignments to such daily details as raising and lowering the flag, checking playground equipment out and back in, and supervising elementary and junior high school playground activities, policing the grounds and overseeing litter removal, providing campus information and escort service to visitors, and so on and on to cover everything the faculty had decided would provide promising pupils an opportunity to develop a sense of responsibility, dependability, imagination, initiative—by all means initiative—and leadership potential.

None of that had ever been any part of anything that Little Buddy Marshall had ever looked forward to. After all, he didn't even like football, basketball, track and field, and tennis, precisely because to him they, unlike baseball and boxing and fishing and hunting and horse-racing and even golf, were schoolboy games and he didn't even want to hear about them.

So naturally you couldn't say anything at all about how you were finding out that the more you knew about geography and history, the better you could read maps and mileage charts and timetables. Not that I was not also the one who had once told him the story I had read about the three princes of Serendip who had set out for a place in particular and had learned to take things as they came. But you couldn't remind him of anything like that either because he may not have actually said, Man, you and them books, Scooter, boy you and them books, but that is what he would have been thinking. So I just let all of that pass but schoolboy (perhaps not beyond but certainly preparatory to anything else) that I had long since become, by that time I couldn't help thinking how much better able to cope with the adventures he was heading for if he already knew as much about the country at large as I did. I could draw a map of the continental boundaries and fill in all the states and capitals and all of the major lakes, rivers, mountains, plains, and deserts, and I could also name and visualize the largest cities and list the principal products and industries.

I said, Goddamn man, and as if he could read my concern, he said, Hey man, remember the good old days you and me used to have. Man, we sure used to have us some times, didn't we, Scooter? And I said, Man, you know it too, and he said, Man, I sure do wish the hell you'd come on and go with me, and I said, Man, you know how bad I want to but, I got to stay here and try to finish up all this stuff first. Because I promised. I promised Mama, man, and I promised Miss Tee and I also promised Old Luze.

I said, You remember that time. But he said, Man, I know what you talking about but that was then. I'm talking about this is now. I'm talking about I don't care what nobody said back then. I talking about I'm *going* this time, don't care what no goddamnbody says.

I didn't say anything else because I knew that you were not going to get anywhere arguing with him. But I didn't really want to try to keep him from saying what he wanted to say, so I just wagged my head with my brows knitted and waited for him to go on, and that's when he said, Man, I didn't really promise Old Luze nothing because I didn't really swear to all that old stuff he was talking about. I just promised him that I wouldn't try to follow *him* no more like that, and I ain't. I just said that because he caught us and he had our ass in a sling and what else could we do? I would've said anything under that bridge that time.

I let that go by also. All I said next was, Aw, man, can't nobody squat back there and call me in there like you, especially with a man on base. And he said, Sheet man, I bet you anything by this next year you going to be ready to get in there and smoke that pill on in there to Old Big Earl himself. Shoot man, you could be on your way to breaking that color line in the goddamn big leagues if it wasn't for them taking up so much of your time with all them old other things over on that old hill.

We were sitting with our legs dangling out of the tailgate of the truck en route to Whistler and as you went on talking, there were also the voices of the other members of the team joking and laughing at the same time, and I can also remember the corridor of overhanging trees and also the power lines along that part of Telegraph Road and how the exhaust fumes used to smell in those days that always become so vivid again no matter where I am when I hear a band playing the channel to "Precious Little Thing Called Love" again. Any time I hear that I also remember how the loose macadamized gravel used to look bouncing along in the red-clay dust the tires kicked back as you rolled on away toward the billboards in the open fields on the outskirts of Chickasaw.

But before we got there we turned off and came on across Kraft Highway which was the only concrete-paved strip to stretch that far beyond the city limits in those days. Then somebody said we were on the Citronelle road and the next turn I remember was the one that brought us into the sandy rut that I always remember when something reminds me of the scrub oaks along the way to the playing field and picnic grounds up to the cypress slope from the Eight Mile Creek swimming place.

That was that June, and we had already played home games against the Box Factory, and the Kelly Hill Nine, and Pine Chapel and had made one trip to Cedar Grove and had also played Chickasaw Terrace in Chickasaw Terrace and also back home. Then on the Fourth of July we played the matinee game in Plateau and as the summer rolled on we also traveled up to Saraland, Chastang, and Mount Vernon and out to Maysville and Oak Grove and also down the coast to Bayou La Batre and Pascagoula.

I don't remember how many games we won and lost that summer, but then there was no pennant to be won anyway because there was no organized league. Your team was tough or maybe about average or a pushover, and that was about it. You sent out letters of challenge which were either accepted or rejected for one reason or another, and most of the games took place on open playing fields to which admission was free and which were kept in regulation playing condition by the players themselves under the supervision of the manager and team captain and usually with the help of a number of faithful fans and sometimes also a few local commercial sponsors.

The main thing about the trip down to Pascagoula was not that we won the seven-inning matinee preliminary and that the adult team lost the big game, but the big dance band from New Orleans playing on a low platform under a wide moss-draped oak near the refreshment stand. They were there for the home team and the number they kept striking up every time their side scored again was "Cake Walking Babies from Home," which I already knew from Miss Blue Eula's record of old Clarence Williams's Blue Five with Louis Armstrong, Sidney Bechet, Charlie Irvis, Buddy Christian, and Eva Taylor.

We spent so much of the rest of the afternoon just hanging around the bandstand that we didn't really try to keep up with what was happening out on the diamond. From where we stood looking and listening, you could read the titles on the music stands and that was the first time I ever saw the score sheets for "Sugar Foot Stomp" and "Royal Garden Blues" which Papa Gladstone's Syncopators had been playing in the Boom Men's Union Hall Ballroom for years.

We didn't get to hear the band from New Orleans play for the big dance that night because as soon as the third man was put out in the top of the ninth inning we had to pile back into the trucks and head back for Mobile and Gasoline Point. But I could hear "Cake Walking Babies" all the way home and it stuck with me all that next week.

But the band tune that Little Buddy Marshall and I always used to hum and whistle because it went with baseball and Gator Gus and also with the Old Luzana Cholly's sporty limp-walk was "Kansas City Stomp" by old sharp dressing, loud woofing Jelly Roll Morton and the Red Hot Peppers. You would also do Old Luzana's sporty limp to Duke Ellington's "Birmingham Breakdown" and years later I was to make his "Cotton Tail" my very own best of all soundtracks for the briar patch. But at that time "Kansas City Stomp" was our theme song. So much so that even to this day, every time I put it on the phonograph I feel the way I used to feel when he was the one and only Little Buddy Marshall he used to be back before he decided that we had come to the parting of the ways.

One day in the middle of that July he said, Man, you don't really believe me when I'm trying to tell you these my last goddamn weeks around these parts, do you Scooter? But you just wait and see if I don't skip on out of here. And I guess I really didn't believe it, or maybe I was just hoping he wouldn't. But I didn't want to talk about it because I didn't even want to think about it anymore.

The last game he and I played together was the one against Oak Grove in Oak Grove. So that was the last time I ever saw him do that old walk-away limp we used to practice to do when you had to slide into home plate. When you got the jump and beat the throw going into second or third, the thing was to hit the dirt and be standing on the bag dusting your hips and hitching up your pants with your forearms while the infielder was still shifting the ball from the glove to his throwing hand. But when you slid into home plate, you always took your time getting up and then you limped a few steps and then you trotted on into the dugout brushing your pants as if it were all just another little detail in a day's work. I had all of that down as well as he did, but he got to do it more often in a real game because he was so much better as a hitter than I ever was to be.

Then sometime during the week before the Labor Day picnic game against Chickasaw Terrace up on the bluffs, he left town one night without saying goodbye, and that was really the end of me and Little Buddy Marshall as running buddies, because when he came back to town that next year just before the end of the school term, he had already been home for almost a week before I found out he was there, and I didn't actually see him until I just happened to meet him coming along the sidewalk from Miss Algenia Nettleton's cookshop.

We stood where we were and talked for about twenty minutes and all he said when I said, Where you been, man, where you been, and what you been up to, was just, Knocking about here and there doing the best I can, man. But I didn't press him because as soon as I saw him I could tell that he was embarrassed and also that he had not yet fully recovered from some illness, which we never came to discuss or even mention.

But when I heard some ten or twelve days later that he had hit the road again, I was not really surprised at all, and the next time I saw him he could hardly wait to tell me about some of the things he had seen and done in such major league baseball cities as Cincinnati and Chicago and St. Louis and Cleveland and Detroit and Pittsburgh, and I said Hey man, eight down and eight to go, because in those days there were eight teams in the National League and eight in the American League. So there were only four more cities to go because St. Louis and Chicago had one in each league and so did Boston and Philadelphia, and New York had the Yankees in the American League and the Giants and the Brooklyn Dodgers in the National League, and Washington had the Senators in the National League. Which, of course, also meant that once you got to any two-league city, say like Chicago with the White Sox and the Cubs, you were where every team in both leagues came to play.

It was almost like old times for a few days during the first part of that summer, and then he said what he said about what had been on his mind about Creola Calloway for all those years and I didn't see him or even hear anything about him for a while and I took it for granted that he had cut out once more. But then a few weeks later there he was again, coming along through Tin Top Alley from Shelby Hill and as soon as he saw me he made his old you-mighty-goddamn-right-I-did gesture and then broke into a few steps of our old sporty-limp strut.

Then not long afterward I found out that he had skipped the city again without saying goodbye, and I guessed that he had headed north by east to Philadelphia and New York and maybe also Boston, and my guess turned out to be true. It also turned out that the day we stopped to talk for a few minutes in Tin Top Alley was the last time I was to see him alive.

The
Briarpatch

XIII

1.

At first I couldn't believe that what was happening to Will Spradley was happening to me, too. After all, when I woke up that morning, I had never heard anything at all about Will Spradley and would not have recognized him as anybody I had ever seen anywhere before. But by sunrise the next day, he had told me about his trouble with Dudley Philpot so many times over and in such personal detail that forever thereafter I was to feel that I had not only been an eyewitness but had also been a party to it step by step, breath by breath.

Will Spradley came plunging headlong and lickety-split through the narrow alley leading from the back of the store, his ears ringing, the pain in his side almost bending him double. *Ain't none of it nothing and here I is, all messed up in the middle of it. All tangled and mangled up in it like this and it ain't nothing and ain't about nothing.*

he was aching all over, and he was breathing blood bubbles

and spitting blood, too, but he was running now, and he had to keep on running. *All of this now. All of this and it ain't nothing, plain flat-out nothing.* He was wet and sticky with blood and sweat, and his legs were stiff, and he could hardly bear to swing his arms. *I ain't done nothing. I ain't said nothing and ain't done nothing. I ain't done nothing to nobody. I ain't never bothered nobody in my life. Everybody know that. You know me, you got to know that.*

he needed to do something about the bleeding and he needed something to hold his side, too, but he couldn't stop for that. Not yet. He couldn't even think about stopping. He had to keep on running and he had to keep on being out of sight, too. Because at least he was this lucky and this far away from that part of it for at least this long. He had to keep on trying. He had to get to Giles Cunningham now. He had to keep on trying and pulling and get there and be there and be gone.

but he had to get there first and let Giles know. *I got to get there so I can tell Gile. I got to let him know. I got to get there and be the one to tell him and clear myself with him because I ain't said nothing about him. I just said what I said because it was true and that's all I meant. I wasn't trying to get him in trouble with nobody. That's what I got to do now. I got to tell him and tell him I didn't want them to get him, too. Because he the one now. He the main one. Because all this ain't nothing to what they going to try to do to him. Because I ain't the one, because I ain't done nothing. He ain't done nothing neither, but he the one. He musta said something. He musta said something terrible.*

he was sucking and spitting blood and the lump around the gash on his cheek had almost closed his eye already. The raw place behind his ear burned all the way to the base of his neck. But he was pulling and pumping with all his might. Not even looking back. Not even daring to look back yet. There wasn't any time to spare to do that yet. Not now. Not yet. Not even with it this dark. He wasn't far enough for that yet. Not even almost.

not even listening back. Not daring to do that either. Because if you looked back, they would be there, and if you listened back, they would be coming, and he had to be getting away from there now, and that was doing this, which was running, which was going, which was leaving, because your second chance was out in front of you now.

because although he couldn't really know what was going to happen next, he knew what he knew about what had already happened, because that part had happened to him, and he knew that even if it had been worse than it had been, which was bad enough, it was still just the beginning. No telling what was going to happen next. Anything could happen now.

he had to get to Giles Cunningham before they got there. *I got to make time. I got to get in and out of there before any of them get there. I got to be somewhere else when they come there. I got to hold out and do this and then I got to find somewheres else to be.*

he had come out of the alley and across that street and cut through the vacant lot where the automobile hulls were. *I got to tell and then I got to be getting further. All of this now. I swear to God, Lord, you never know.* He was coming to the next street then. And then he was across that one, too, and he was crawling through the fence and into the pecan orchard and coming on through there.

it had been raining off and on all day, and the ground was wet and the air was damp, and there was a thin mist among the trees and the night shapes again. It was going to be chilly again but the dampness was still warm now. It was hot to him. His breath was hot, his collar was hot, and his clothes were almost steaming.

he made it to the next fence and got through the railing and was crawling on through there, too, his arms and legs numb now, his head splitting with pain. The whole left side of his face was swollen out of shape, and he could hardly see out of his left eye. He could hardly hear out of his left ear, and every time he stretched too far the pain in his side almost took his breath away.

he was crawling along the garden furrow to get to the next

fence, and then he would be at that road. Then he would be coming along there. If they didn't cut him off and hem him in and catch him anywhere along there, he would have a chance to make it to that corner, which was where that part of town began. He was headed for the edge of town and the railroad, but he had to get through here first, and then Higgins Quarters and the lumberyard.

he was running again then, and he had to keep on running until he was there. *If I slow down, I'll be tired. If I slow down, I won't be able to run no more, and I can't make it, and I got to, because I got to get there and tell Gile because I'm the cause of it, but it ain't my fault. It ain't my fault because it ain't nothing no how, and God knows I ain't done a thing.*

he came staving on along the footpath beside the wide, curving road, running in the open, exposed in all directions now, his whole being straining with alertness. He had to be ready to jump in a split second. *I got to hear good now and hear them before I see them because if I don't, they got me.*

the main thing was automobiles, especially coming from behind. If you didn't hear the motor before the headlights came, the beams would hit you in the back and it would be like a charge of buckshot between the shoulder blades. If that happened, it would be too late. If that happened, they would have him again, and it wouldn't be just one but all of them this time. He would have to be there and they would be there all around him, and anything could happen.

that would be here; it would be happening right here. *And ain't none of them got nothing to do with it because it ain't nothing no how. Ain't got nothing to do with it and don't even know nothing about what it's all about, don't know the first thing about none of it. All this time now, and now all of this. But they ain't thinking about that. They don't want to know about that, don't need to know. They ain't going to be asking no questions because they ain't going to be needing no answers. Because I'm the only answer they want now, me and Gile, and it's more Gile than me, because he's really the one, but if they get me it's me, too, and here I is ain't done nothing to nobody.*

everything depended on how lucky he was now. That was all he had to go on now, because all he could do was try to keep on doing what he was doing right now, which was this, which was running, which was all numbness now and pulling, which was pumping, his chest tight, his breath raw, the dull cramp in his side getting sharper and sharper all the time. *I got to outrun this now. This ketch in my side. If I keep on it'll go away. I got to get rid of this and get my second wind. When I get my second wind, I'll feel better and I can make better time. I got to make better time than this. A whole lot better.*

he came lunging on, and then he was there in that part of town which was the last part, and he had to slow down because he had to be ready to break from shadow to shadow now. *This far now. And now I got to get through here.* He was running narrow then. *I got to make it on through here, and get to the lumberyard and get on through there and make it all the way. I can't let them get me now. All of them now, and just me out here all by myself. All over something like that, and it ain't even nothing.* He came darting on, running not on strength but on necessity now, because although it had all started about something which was really nothing in the first place, it was about everything and everybody now. And all he knew about what was going to happen next was that anything could happen, and once it got started there was no telling where it was going to stop.

he came grinding on and the main thing was the numbness. It wasn't the pain anymore. It was the dull bumping numbness and the way his stomach was. *If I can just make it on past there and make it on to that sweet gum I can make it. I got to make it that far now. I got to make it that far and I'll have me a good head start then, and I can make it on through there.*

I shoulda knowed better and I did. Ain't no use in them saying that, because I did, and I was doing everything in my power to do and I sure God did everything he said and he know it, and then he started all of that about something like that and I couldn't do nothing after that.

because it was happening too fast from then on. Everything had been going along all that time and then all of a sudden it had changed to that and there he was right in the middle of it, all hemmed up in the very middle of it. He couldn't do anything right because he couldn't even believe it that quick. He saw it happening and he knew it was happening but he couldn't believe it because he was too stunned to believe it. Because he was dumbfounded, flabbergasted. Because there he was and there it was happening before he could even get started on what he was going to say, before he could even get set to start thinking about all of the things he knew he had to try to say, and then it was too late.

he had known good and well that it could happen, but somehow he just couldn't believe that it was going to happen that fast, and all of a sudden it was like a steel trap springing shut on you. That was enough to shock anybody. That was enough to paralyze you. Because there you were and it was like a bear trap or something and you knew it and you knew you had to unbait it, and you were trying and there you were being as careful as anybody could be and all of a sudden it had sprung before you could even touch it.

but what had really stunned him was the fact that he had forgotten what it was like, because he was shocked but he was not really surprised. It hadn't really surprised him. Because surprises come out of the clear blue sky, and this was not like that at all, because he had been living knowing it could happen almost all of his life, and knowing that long was waiting that long, too. But he had forgotten it, too, because he had been so busy trying to keep it from happening that he had forgotten all about what it really was, and all of a sudden there it was and it was him and this: *him facing Dudley Philpot, and Dudley Philpot holding the pistol.*

2.

I told him and that didn't do no good at all. I told him and he just kept right on. He knew it wasn't my fault and he come lighting into me like that. Just like I was the one and he know good and well it wasn't none of me. I told him I couldn't help it, and he know Gile Cunningham as good as I do. I come right straight on there and told him just as soon as it happened and if he was going to do something he ought to done it then, but all he done was just say that then and I thought I was out of it. I thought he was just going to say that and let me go on and he did and I thought that was it. He wouldn't let me give it to him and he said for me to tell Gile and I did and I figured it was him and Gile then, and it was, and then he come sending for me again and I thought it was all over and done with. I just thought he was ready to take it and let me go on then and here he come with all of this. Just like I ain't had it at all and I had it right there for him to take in the first place. All of this about something like that and I had it right there and he wouldn't let me give it to him, like what difference did that make. All this now and I still ain't give it to him and I had it all the confound time.

he made it on past Neely's Crossing and came on until he saw the sweet gum tree, and then he left the railroad and came on down across the right-of-way to where he knew the trail began. He had to slow down and catch his breath then, but he couldn't stop. He was trotting and then he was walking, and then he was trotting again.

I tried to tell that crazy fool, trouble-making Gile, he said to himself without realizing it. I tried to tell him and that didn't do no good at all. I told him. I said, look, Gile, I got to do that first, and he didn't pay that no attention at all. He made me do it. He made me. He had me and I told him and he made me do it anyhow. He had me then and what else could I do and there I was then and all I could do was go on and I did and I was going along that street and I came on past the sweet shrubs and the warehouse, and then I slowed back down again because I was almost there and I had to think about what I was going to tell him because it wasn't nothing, but I knew good and well he wasn't going to like it and he sure God didn't.

Then I was there and I went on through the store to the office, and he was busy talking to old man Cliff from the secondhand store up the street. Standing there leaning back against the front edge of the desk smoking, looking down at their feet, and then he saw me and looked at me and I waited, and I was still trying to think up something but all I was doing was waiting, and then old man Secondhand Cliff was gone and I was standing there with my hat, like that, and he was sitting in the swivel chair behind the desk again.

"Well, Will?"

"How you, Mister Dub?" I said.

"Pretty good, Will. How you?"

"Not so good, Mister Dub," I said.

"Well, let's see now." He said that like he always did and I heard it and heard that kind of breathing that goes with that kind of talk, and I was thinking, that's the way white folks talk, they have noses like that and they breathe like that when they talk.

"Mister Dub," I said.

"Just a minute, Will," and he took the key from his pocket and opened the drawer and took out that little old checker-back school tablet. Then he took out the metal box.

"Mister Dub," I said.

"All right, Will."

Then I took the money from my watch pocket and unfolded it.

"Take it out of this, Mister Dub," I said.

"Where's that check, Will?"

"I ain't got it, Mister Dub," I said.

"You ain't got it?"

"No, sir," I said, "not this time."

"Well, where the hell is it then, Will?"

"Sir?"

"Where'd you get all that cash money from, Will?"

"Well, you see, Mister Dub, I had another little transaction. I had to take care of that," I said.

"But what are you doing with all that cash money, Will?"

"He cashed it, Mister Dub," I told him.

"Who cashed it, Will?"

"Gile Cunningham, Mister Dub," I said.

"Giles Cunningham?"

"Yes, sir," I said.

"What the hell is that nigger doing cashing your checks, Will?"

"Well, sir, you see I owed him a little something, too, and I was on my way here but I kinda bumped into him first."

"You know I'm the one that cashes your checks, Will."

That's how it started. About nothing, and all I could think about then was all this about a percent. So he can deduct that measly percent and a quarter for surcharge. Gile didn't charge me nothing for cashing it. I did not look at him then, because I know good and well what was coming. I didn't say nothing.

"You know that, Will," he said, not looking at me. I wasn't looking at him either, but I saw him.

"But I got your money, Mister Dub," I said. "I was on my way here."

"Didn't you tell him I cash your checks for you?" he asked.

"Yes, sir. I told him," I said.

"Well, what the hell did he cash it for then?"

"I don't know, sir, Mister Dub. I told him."

"You sure you told him?"

"Yes, sir. I'm dead sure, Mister Dub. But you know Gile Cunningham, Mister Dub."

"You get out of here and get it back."

"But he on his way out of town, Mister Dub. That's how come he done it, anyhow."

"*Well, you get out there and catch him and tell him I say send that damn check in here.*"

"*But he already gone, Mister Dub.*"

"*You get out of here and don't come back till you get it.*"

"*Yes, sir, but he gone for four or five days.*"

"*Where'd he go?*"

"*I don't know, sir, Mister Dub. He didn't tell me that.*"

"*Well, you get ahold of him as soon as he gets back and bring that check in here.*"

"*But I can't make him give it to me, Mister Dub. You know Gile Cunningham, Mister Dub. You know how he is.*"

"*Well, goddamn it, you tell that black son-of-a-bitching bastard I say bring it in here hisself or you tell him I say his black ass'll wish he had.*"

"*He didn't mean you no harm or nothing like that, Mister Dub,*" I said.

"*You tell him what I said.*"

All I said then was, "Yessir," and I didn't spend a single penny of my own money all that time. My own money now. Mamie and them gone back out to Indian Stand again and all that. All because of that and all of it is just about as near nothing as anything I ever heard tell of in my life. Me waiting around all that time now.

And then as soon as I come back in there and seen his face like that I could tell what had happened and I already knowed, anyhow. Because I know Gile Cunningham and I know Gile Cunningham don't care, trouble or no trouble, and he ain't never been one to bite his tongue for nobody and everybody know it. White folks know that just like everybody else and that's why don't none of them do nothing but look at him and leave him alone. Gile Cunningham don't care nothing about no two-bit peckerwood like no Dub Philpot.

As soon as I come in and seen his face like that, I knowed I was in for it, and I knowed just about what had happened. I had been hoping all day that it was going to be all over, but I knowed that it was just beginning then.

3.

He had been standing there looking toward Dud Philpot then. Knowing that he himself was being looked up and down, but he didn't look him back in the eye. Because he knew white folks and he knew they didn't like for you to do that. They thought you might be figuring on doing something if you did that, and that made them uneasy and there was no telling what they were liable to do to you then. But he was watching him and he could also feel him and he could sense every move he might make as soon as it started. He was waiting then, and then he realized that he was supposed to start talking first.

"I come as soon as I got your word, Mister Dub, and I brung the money too. I was right over yonder at the cab stand waiting all the time I been over there all day."

"What did I tell you to do?"

"When, Mister Dub?"

Will Spradley had moved his feet then. He mad now. He good and mad now. He getting ready to raise hell now. He bound to raise holy hell now. All about a measly little percent. All because Gile done that and then he couldn't make him do what he said. He got to raise hell now.

"I done what you told me, Mister Dub," he had said. "I told him what you told me to."

"I told you to bring that goddamn check in here in the first place."

"Yes, sir," he had said.

"Didn't I tell you?"

"Yes, sir. You sure did, Mister Dub."

Dud Philpot had been sitting, holding the desk, looking at him then, gripping it harder and harder every time he spoke, his face getting redder, his knuckles whiter; and Will Spradley wanted to say something to calm him down but he couldn't think of it fast enough then, and the next thing he knew Philpot was standing up.

"Yes, sir, Mister Dub, you sure did."

"Goddamnit, I'm beginning to believe you think you're getting smart, Will Spradley. Trying me. You and that Giles."

"No, sir, Mister Dub, nothing like that, Mister Dub. No sir, Mister Dub, not me."

His eyes were narrow then and he was breathing, coming close, and his neck and ears were getting redder and redder, and he was glaring, and then all of a sudden he started to shake all over as if it had just come to him what he was angry about.

Will Spradley had moved about again then, watching him without really looking at him. He going to start something now. He bound to start something now. Just as sure as I'm standing here. Just as sure as rain and I'm here. White folks. He had moved again then, but he didn't really move, he just didn't stand still.

"It was just a mistake, Mister Dub. Gile Cunningham, he—"

"Goddamn your black nigger soul to hell." Dud Philpot struck at him then, reaching, swinging across the desk, but Will Spradley moved, almost without moving, and Philpot missed him and almost lost his balance.

"Aw, Mister Dub, ain't no use of that."

Philpot was halfway around the desk then and he swung again, but Will Spradley twisted to one side and took that blow with his elbow up in front of his face, and began backing away, and then he turned to make a break for the door. But before he could make it there, Philpot had leapt back to the desk and snatched the pistol from the already open top drawer and leveled it at him.

"Make one more move, you black-livered bastard, and I'll blow your nigger brains out. You hear me nigger? Do you hear me, you sneaky black son-of-a-bitch?"

"Mister Dub, I ain't done nothing. I ain't done a thing! What did I do, Mister Dub? You know me, Mister Dub."

Will Spradley was coming slowly on back toward him then. He got me now. He got me. Goddamn that goddamn trouble-making Gile Cunningham. And ain't nothing I can do because then where would I be? All the people in this town and it's got to be me, and he know good and well it ain't me.

"You know me, Mister Dub."

Dud Philpot changed the pistol to his left hand then and swung his right but missed him and lost his balance again, and Will Spradley jumped forward to keep him from going down and jumped back, realizing that he had touched him.

"Aw, Mister Dub."

Dud Philpot slapped him again then, forehand and backhand.

"I'll teach you."

"I ain't done nothing, Mister Dub. You been knowing me all this time, Mister Dub. You know that, Mister Dub."

"Shut up!"

"But Mister Dub—"

That was when Dud Philpot began hitting him with the pistol.

"What you going to do, Mister Dub? I ain't done nothing, I ain't done a thing. What you going to do, Mister Dub?"

Dud Philpot struck him a gashing swipe on the side of his head with the barrel then, and Will Spradley staggered, watching him through the blood and fell and started crawling toward the door.

"Please, Mister Dub, please, sir," *he said, but he knew that Dud Philpot was getting too tired to raise the pistol again.*

"I told you not to move."

That was when he kicked him. It was not strong enough to hurt, but Will Spradley pitched himself forward into a sprawl.

"Get up!" *Dud Philpot's voice was almost a whisper.*

But Will Spradley didn't get up any further than his knees, and he kept his legs together and held one arm around his stomach and the other hand before his blood-streaked face. I said, Please, sir, and he still doing it. I told him please sir, because he got me and he know it. I could get him, too, but I can't because then it would be all that. I could do it right now if I wanted to. I could ram him right now and grab him and turn him every way but aloose. He ain't thought about that. He so worked up, he forgot about that. I could grab him right now. All I got to do is ram right on into him. Lord, don't let him think about that now. He surely kill me if he think about that. If he think about that, I'm gone and ain't nobody going to do nothing either. White folks.

"Please don't, Mister Dub," he said in a falsetto that was no less deliberate than habitual. "Please have mercy, Mister Dub. Oh Lord, Jesus, have mercy, Mister Dub."

Dud Philpot had started kicking him again then, but he had to stop and catch his breath every time, and at first all Will Spradley had done was keep himself covered as he was and wait.

I said please and he was still doing it, but I was pretty sure he wasn't going to shoot me and he was too tired to aim straight anyhow, and I was thinking it was almost over because he was too tired and weak to be mad, because he was so tired he was going to have to start thinking about it and remember it wasn't me because he knew—good and well knew—it was Gile. So he had doubled over, hoping that would hurry it because he had to get somewhere and get the bleeding stopped.

But the next kick had not come and that was when he had suddenly realized how much danger he was really in. That's the part that really scared me and I was hauling out of there and out here before I knew it, gun or no gun, because I could hear him just standing there huffing and puffing like that, and I knew if he fainted it was going to be me if he come to saying I did it and if he didn't come to, I didn't have no chance at all. White folks. White folks. White folks. But now I got to get there and tell Gile.

And black ones, too. Yeah, them too. Goddamn right, them too. Because ain't no use of them saying that because that don't make me that, just because I didn't do that. They can call me anything they want to, but anybody say I'm that don't know what they talking about. That's all right with me because goddamn the luck I know they going to say it anyhow, because all

I want to do now is get there and tell Gile. They can say anything they goddamn want to.

he came on and on and on pulling against the pain and pumping against the stiffness and the swelling and then he had his second wind and his second chance. But he still couldn't really believe it was happening to him.

XIV

Not that I didn't already know people like Will Spradley. I have always known and heard about people like him. But I must say that it has also been my good fortune to have also always known quite a few who could easily have been very much like him but were not. There was Ed Riggins, for instance, better known as Evil Ed Riggins and perhaps even better as Old Man Evil Ed. By which people of all persuasions in and around Gasoline Point meant that he was not only somewhat foul-mouthed as if on principle but also downright badassed when crossed.

He was one I was to find myself remembering again as soon as I realized what turn the story Will Spradley was telling me was about to take. Any time his name used to be mentioned around the fireside or on the swing porch, somebody always had to say something about how he never was one to take any stuff from anybody, especially white people, whom he almost always called white folks. Even when he was addressing them individually, he would say, What say white folks or, Howdo white folks or say, Lookahere white folks and so on, and he was the one who referred to important looking white women not as Miss Ann or Miss Lady but as Miss I Am, as in "Look at Miss I Am up there, call herself clerking on that typing machine. White folks, white folks, white folks. I declare to God!"

Everybody knew the one about how he used to signify at his own boss man back in the old days up in the farming country before moving down into Mobile County during the wartime shipbuilding boom in Chickasaw. All you had to do was be somewhere sometime as I was in the barbershop that time when somebody reminded him of Old Man Jake Turner Cuthbert.

Whoever it was went on to say, I remember one time when damn near half the farm folks in that district was still standing around that little old two-by-four crossroads town after dark, waiting for old man Jake to get back from the county seat with the payroll. You remember that, Ed? And Old Ed Riggins said, Goddamn right I remember it and all them old hunch-shouldered, boney-butt peckerwoods standing around everywhere waiting for him, too, just like us, and I'm the one got to tell him. I said, Where the hell is that goddamn old white man with my money I done sweated all the week for? I said, This is Sadday night. I said, I done give him the time he hire me for and now this here is my goddamn time he messing with. He ain't paying me for this and look at all these stores still open so people can settle up a few things and pick up a little something and get on home. Goddamn.

And I told him, too. I said, Man, where you been, white man, just coming in here this time of night? I said, Man, you know this is Sadday. And he come talking about nigger, and I said, Man, nigger nothing. I said, Business is business. I said, Nigger ain't got nothing to do with this. I said, What about all these old hungry white folks around here? Just like everybody else. And he said, Yeah, but nigger. And I said, Man, how you going to nigger your way out of something like this? I said, You know good and well I am eating out of a paper sack. I said, You the one eating out of the cupboard, not me and these people. I said, I'm eating out of a paper sack one can at a time.

I also knew what people in Gasoline Point meant when they said Old Evil Ed Riggins *didn't even lower his voice in the bank* because I was there one day when he came in. It was not that he was loud. He wasn't. But when he spoke in his normal tone of voice, you suddenly realized that the tone everybody else was using was hardly above a whisper and also that they were moving about as if they were not only in church but at a funeral.

As a matter of fact, he didn't even raise his voice when you saw him standing somewhere signifying at everybody in earshot as I came upon him doing at the entrance to Hammel's Department Store one day. When he said, Well, let me get on in here and see if I can figure out what these old Mobile, Alabama, white folks coming up with this time, he was not really trying to get attention. He was only thinking aloud in public and signifying and scandalizing anybody who happened to be listening.

He also used to like to say, You damn sure better be on your goddamn p's and q's because you can bet your bottom dollar these old goddamn white folks going to be trying to come up with something else, and damn if I believe they know what the hell it is they own selves most of the goddamn time, if you want to know the goddamn truth. Hell, it ain't my goddamn fault. I didn't make them. I'm just trying to find out how to deal with these we got around here.

People used to say he walked with one shoulder hunched just slightly higher than the other because he was so used to wearing an underarm holster for his 38 Special and that when the weather was too warm for a coat or his stiffly starched blue denim overall jumper-jacket, you could tell by a little added drag in his sporty walk that he was carrying his back-up Derringer in a leg holster.

He had started out up in the country as a turpentine worker.

Then he had become a woodsman and hunting guide. That was how he got his reputation as the dead-eye pump gun and Winchester expert, bar none. He still hunted bear and deer as well as rabbits, possum, squirrels, and coons, ducks, and quail and now he also had a rowboat that he used not only for channel fishing but also for bagging ducks, marsh hens, and wild guineas up in Hog Bayou (which was also wild boar and alligator territory) and over in the canebrakes of Pole Cat Bay.

The only explanation I ever heard anybody give for the way he always woofed and signified wherever he was around white people was that it was what he did to keep *everybody* reminded that no matter who you were, he was not the kind of man you could mess with and expect to get away with it. Nobody I ever asked or overheard around the fireside, on the swing porch, or in the barbershop or anywhere else ever claimed to know about any specific occurrence that it all could be traced back to. Nor could anybody name anybody anywhere who ever called his hand.

I did know who Dudley Philpot was when I woke up that morning but only by name because of the sign on the front of his store, which I had never set foot inside of but which I knew was about a half of a block off Courthouse Square going toward Carmichael Construction Supply Company. I did not know him by sight and I had never wondered what he was like because he didn't have any kind of reputation that I had ever heard anything about.

Giles Cunningham, on the other hand, was somebody I already knew by sight as well as reputation. I had never actually met him, but I became used to seeing him in the barbershop and on the block during the past three years, and so I had also picked up enough information about him (most of it casual and incidental) to know that he owned the Dolomite Ballroom out near Montgomery Fork, the hillside eating place called the Pit (as in barbecue pit), a short distance out of town on U.S. 80 going toward the Georgia state line, and that the Plum (as in plum thickets and also as in plumb out of town and nearly out of the country), the after-hours spot off Route 33 going south by east to the Florida panhandle, belonged to him.

By the time that I had become the upperclassman and prospective honor graduate that I was when I woke up that morning, I had also learned enough about him to know that he also owned two subdivisions, one near the campus and another out in the hill section where he lived, that he owned a chicken farm and fourteen hundred acres of farmland out in the country, and that he also had part ownership in several other concerns, including a dry-cleaning business which a cousin was operating in Chattanooga and a bay-front resort and fishing camp which his half-brother was getting started down below Mobile and Dog River.

I also knew that his houseman at the ballroom was Wiley Payton, an old trench buddy from the AEF and that one Speck (as in Speckle Red) Jenkins, an old L & N dining car chef out of Montgomery, took care of the day-to-day details at the Pit and that the man in charge out at the Plum was one Flea (for Fleetwood) Mosley, an old pre-Prohibition bartender and off-time pool shark from Birmingham.

Along with the ballroom into which headline road bands were booked once or twice a week, the Dolomite also had a big bar off the main lobby that was open every night and had its own combo and a floor show. The Pit was strictly an eating place that was open for breakfast and closed after dinner, which was served from 5:30 to 8:30 P.M. on weekdays and 5:30 to midnight on Saturdays. The Plum was an old-time down-home jook joint with a honky-tonk piano player named Gits Coleman.

The Pit was also his headquarters. So that was where he spent most of his time during daylight hours and that was where you called to get him on the phone. He also spent a certain amount of time at the other places, too, but anybody trying to get in touch with him always called the Pit first. Some people also knew that in case of an emergency, you could also get a message to him by calling Hortense Hightower.

He made a daily check of the Dolomite and the Plum either in the morning or early afternoon while things were being set up and then again at night when everything was supposed to be rolling. Sometimes he ran out to the poultry farm once a week and sometimes twice. Otherwise, he left everything up there to Ed Mitchell, a graduate from the School of Agriculture, who sent eggs and dressed chickens into the Pit and also to the clubs. The only time he made regular trips to his other farms further out in the country was during the planting and harvest seasons. Otherwise, he seldom went more than once every two or three weeks.

You could also find him in town for a while every morning because he usually went to the bank before noon, and when Wiley Peyton wasn't with him during that part of the day, it was usually Flea Mosley, and unless there was some reason to check by the courthouse, the next stop was always his office at the Pit because that was where he usually took care of bills and orders. He always put in the big orders himself, and he also booked all the name bands and personally produced and promoted all of the special dances and coordinated the annual galas sponsored by the local social clubs.

As a matter of fact, Giles Cunningham and the Pit and the Dolomite and the Plum (and thus also Wiley Peyton and Flea Mosley and Speck Jenkins) were all very much a part of what was on my mind when I woke up that morning, because as soon as I realized that I was no longer asleep and remembered what day it was, I began thinking about Hortense Hightower and the way she had said what she said.

After all, I had already found out most of what I knew about him and his concerns long before I had finally come to realize that she herself even existed. Nor had I just been hearing about him. I had actually been seeing him at fairly close range although not with any one-on-one personal familiarity ever since the first term of my freshman year because he always came on the block at least once a week. He was always there every Friday afternoon, the big black Cadillac parked head on into the curb in front of the barbershop.

That was when Skeeter always got him ready for the weekend. That included a hair trim, shampoo, shave, and facial, and there was also a manicurist on Friday and Saturday. Sometimes when all of that was over, he would also hang around for a while swapping lies and signifying with Deke Whatley, the owner, or he would come back out and stand in front of Red's Varsity Threads next door, talking sports with Red Gilmore.

You couldn't miss him, standing with one leg dropped back like that, the toes of his highly glossed, elegantly narrow, and thin-soled shoes pointing inward, shoulders erect but with the left ever so slightly lower than the right and with his hat, which always looked brand new, and which he wore tilted toward his left brow, blocked long with the brim turned up all around in what I used to call the Birmingham/Kansas City poolroom homburg style.

Whatever he was wearing always went well with his barbershop-smooth ginger-brown skin and the way he handled himself. He was just about six feet even, solidly built but with a little bulge in the midsection that along with his smartly hand-tailored hand-finished suits and custom-made shirts and accessories made him look more like a road musician or gambler who might go hunting and fishing from time to time than like an athlete.

But as I found out early on, he had started out to be a prize fighter, another Jack Johnson, and heavyweight champion of the world. A lot of boys were going to be another Jack Johnson or another Joe Gans back in those days, and he made a pretty good start and he had kept it up when he was conscripted and sent to camp. But when they shipped him overseas, he got a chance to see another part of the world and all of that had given him a lot of other possibilities to consider.

He had not really been old enough to be called up, but he looked more adult than he was at the time, and he had been putting his age up so that he could hang around the saloons and pool halls so he was drafted and he fought in the Vosges mountains and also in the Argonne forest, and he had had himself some fun over there, too. He had lied to go AWOL to get into Paris, but he and Wiley Peyton had made it there three times. He and Wiley Peyton had been in the same company from the very outset and by the time they reached the embarkation point of Newport News, Virginia, they were buddies, so they had gone on to do a lot of French towns together just as they had done their share of going over the top and through the barbwire together.

When he came back stateside, he had started running on the L & N as a Pullman porter and had also become a dining car headwaiter, and that was when he really began to pick up on how you made good money by providing first-class service. And then he went to Harlem during the boom in the 1920s and got a job in a big midtown hotel, and that's when he decided what he wanted to do and started putting money aside and laying his plans.

Then when the big Depression struck at the end of the decade, he took what he had saved, along with all of the tricks of the trade that he had picked up from the railroad and New York by that time, and came on back down home and went into business for himself, starting with the Pit, which was just another old run-down roadside chicken shack when he made his downpayment on it.

XV

She said, Hi there, Schoolboy, and I could have said not for very much longer. Because it was already the middle of that third January and I was less than five months away from being a senior, and then there would be the summer and I would be on my way to what comes after commencement. But I didn't say that. I said, I don't deny my name. I said, I don't deny my name because going to school is still my game. And she had to smile and then she winked and said, I don't deny my name either, Schoolboy, and sat on the next stool with her back to the bar.

That was how I met Hortense Hightower. I already knew who she was. Everybody present knew who she was because she was the main attraction in that wing of the Dolomite complex. She was the singer the five-piece combo was there to play behind, and she was also the dancer featured in the Friday and Saturday night floor shows, which also included a chorus line of six dancers who doubled as backup singers, a comedian named Gutbucket, and also a guest spot for a singer or instrumentalist.

All I actually knew about her at that time was how she sounded and the way she came across on stage and what a good-looking, svelte, nutmeg-brown woman she was. I had not yet found out anything at all about where she had grown up and where she had worked before. I knew that she had been in town for five or six years, but I hadn't ever seen her in person until that last Christmas break when I finally went along with Marcus Bailey and Clifton Jackson, two fellow upperclassmen from Birmingham who made the rounds of all the outlying joints several times a month.

On all of my other trips out to the club before then, I had always been in such a big rush to get inside the main hall to get as close as possible to the musicians in the big-name bands that came through on tour that I never had paid any attention at all to the ongoing local entertainment in the after-hours room on your left as you came into the main lobby. After all, the name bands such as Duke Ellington, Jimmie Lunceford, Count Basie, and others that you heard on the radio and on records (and also some of the territory bands like, say, the Sunset Royals) were something you scrimped and saved up for.

She sang some new and some standard pop songs. She sang the blues in all tempos, and she would also do a torch song on request. But you could tell that she got a special kick out of swinging love songs like "My Blue Heaven," "I Can't Believe That You're in Love with Me," and "Exactly Like You" off-time to a medium tempo, and as soon as you heard her shout one twelve-bar chorus with the combo signifying back at her over an ever-steady, omni-flexible, four/four, you knew exactly why they called her Boss Lady.

Not that she was ever actually bossy, not in the least. She didn't have to be. Her authority was as casual as it was complete. All she had to do was come tripping on stage with the combo riffing "At Sundown," and it was as if the storybook queen herself had just entered the throne room, and when she bowed and smiled and waited for everything to settle down, it was (for me at any rate and perhaps on some level of feeling if not quite of consciousness for others, too) almost as if it were about to be Mother Goose tale time around the fireside once more. *Schoolboy that I was and to some extent still am, that was what came to mind at the very outset of the first show I saw her open and just as I was about to whisper to Marcus and Clayton that there were few things anywhere in the world better with some down-home bootleg ale than a good-looking brown-skinned woman with another blue-steel fairy tale, there were the drum rolls, the piano vamping, and her opening proclamation: Let's drink some mash and talk some trash this evening.*

On stage she came across as a seasoned professional at ease and in charge, but sitting next to her at the bar you could see that she was probably not yet in her midthirties, if she was yet thirty, and you also realized that she had seemed taller on stage because she had long-looking, rubbery-nimble legs and she also moved like the dancer she also was. From that alone I guessed that she was size fourteen (36″-24″-38″), which in those days used to mean that along with everything else she was built for speed and maneuverability and also stacked for heavy duty and endurance. It was not until later on that I began saying that she was bass clef, although I had already picked that up from my brand-new roommate during the very first term of my freshman year.

You could also see how little stage makeup she needed for a room that size, and you could tell that the high sheen of her long black wavy hair, which she wore pulled back and clamped into a ponytail, did not come from a hot-comb treatment. All it took was a very small amount of a very light oil and a few routine strokes with a regular dressing-table comb-and-brush set.

I saw you listening, she said, and when she smiled at that range you got a quick flash of one gold filling that looked more like a cosmetic touch than a necessary correction because the rest of her teeth were without any visible flaws at all. And so were her hands and fingers, which, like those of so many brown-skin women I remember over the years, were every bit as small and elegantly tapered as I have always imagined that those of storybook princesses, being of regal birth, were expected to be.

This is not your first time in here, she said, and I said, My third time, my second time on my own, but before she could say anything else somebody cut in to say something nice and give her a show-biz hug and a fake kiss and then there was a couple who did the same thing, and when they left she said, A lot of college boys come in here all the time, but you're the first one I spotted sitting back here all by himself listening with your ear cocked like that, so I said, Who is that one and where did he come from?

So where do you come from, Schoolboy, she said, and when I told her, she said, I've been down through there more than once. So you grew up hearing Old Papa Gladstone and y'all must have more jook joints on the outskirts of Mobile than any other town in this state.

She herself was from Anniston by way of Bessemer, she said, and within the next week or so she also told me about how she had started out in the church choir in Anniston and had become a soloist by the time she was a teenager. She had finished high school in Bessemer and won a scholarship to 'Bama State, but she had dropped out after a year to join a road band barnstorming through the Alabama, Florida, Georgia, Mississippi territory. That was when she became a dancer because the bandleader wanted her to be an all-round entertainer as well as a singer. And for a while she had also played around with the idea of becoming a headliner with her own road show.

When it was time for her to get ready to go back on stage, she stood up and put her hand out and as I took it she said, A lot of college boys come in here all the time, but you're the first one I spotted listening like that, so I just decided to come over here and say something to you and find out what you're putting down. And I said, I sure am glad you did, but what did you find out? and she said, A whole lot. I can usually tell a lot about people from what I see from up there, and it usually don't take me but so many more bars to check them out close up.

Then as she stepped back to head for her dressing room, she gave me a playful one-finger push on the shoulder and said, You just checked out just fine, Schoolboy. I do believe that you just might do. Then, before I could get myself together to say something cute, she winked and waved and was gone and I couldn't believe my luck.

XVI

So when I finally let myself take time out to think about her again that next morning, I said, Hello, Miss Hortense Hightower, whichever you are. Because I was also thinking about the one and only Miss Slick McGinnis, also known as Slick to some and as Old Slick to others, so-called not because she was so notoriously devious but from the time when she used to wear her hair bobbed and plastered flapper style. The fact that she always looked at you as if she knew more than she would ever tell and as if she always meant more than she ever actually said was really a coincidence after the fact.

She had been right there all along, although not all the time because she also traveled a lot. So much so that whenever you saw her it was as if she had either just recently come back down home from New York City and sometimes elsewhere as well. Or she was only a few days away from going back off again. Or so it seemed. But even so, everybody always used to think of her as being as much of an ongoing part of whatever took place in Gasoline Point in those days as anybody else. And so did I and so did she.

Most of the time she used to be going back and forth between Gasoline Point and New York, but sometimes you also used to hear people talking about something she had brought back from Paris, France, or London, England, or Rome, Italy, or Madrid, Spain, where she, like Jack Johnson, had not only seen but had also met some of the world's greatest bullfighters and had also heard a lot of great gypsy guitar players and had also seen a lot of flamenco dancing which I had also seen on the Spanish floats in the Mardi Gras parade which is why I already knew the difference between the sounds of castanets and the syncopated riffing of the old plantation-style bone-knockers and thigh-slappers you used to hear on street corners in those days.

At first I used to remember her as the pretty lady with the spangle-dangle ear pendants, diamond ring, and string of pearls, who sometimes also sported a cigarette holder that was said to be platinum and ivory. Then later the sound of whatever shoes she happened to be wearing as she came clip-clopping along the sidewalk always used to make me think of bunny-pink bedroom mules and boa-trimmed kimonos.

I always knew that she had been married for a while a few years ago, but didn't have any children, and all anybody seemed to know about her ex-husband was that he was somebody who ran some kind of business up in New York, who refused to come down South even on a week's vacation. So nobody in Gasoline Point, not even his in-laws, had ever seen him in the flesh, which probably was why nobody ever thought of him as an actual person anymore. He was only a shadowy part of a half-forgotten event that in itself was not very real to anybody in the first place. Anyway, by the time I was old enough to become just casually curious about who he was and what his line of work was, nobody could tell you or could remember what his name was (it was not McGinnis, to be sure). Or could say if anybody else in Gasoline Point other than Miss Slick McGinnis and her family ever knew what it was.

I also don't remember having already known anything about what she herself had been doing for a living all of those years before she decided to tell me what she told me after I had answered the questions she asked me about school the day I helped her carry her parcels home from the post office. Before then I didn't have any notion whatsoever that she had a very special job with a very rich high society woman who lived in New York and traveled all over the world. All I knew was that from time to time she traveled a lot.

Then during the next several weeks I was to find out that the high society New York woman she had been working for and who was responsible for her being up north when she went was somebody who was once her blonde blue-eyed playmate back when the McGinnis family was living in the truck-gardening area across Mobile Bay near the resort town of Daphne.

That was another story in itself, one about how the blonde blue-eyed playmate, whose family was in the drydock business, grew up to be one of the most popular debutantes in the whole Gulf Coast region and about how she married into a family in the shipbuilding industry in New York, and then it was also a story about a mansion on Fifth Avenue and an estate on Long Island with stables and kennels and about a family yacht for sailing the Atlantic and cruising the Mediterranean and the Aegean, and also about how Miss Slick McGinnis had always been able to spend so much time back down in Gasoline Point.

But that was not what we really talked about that first afternoon. All she told me then was that the packages were from some people she lived with up in New York, and then from what she said from time to time later on I found out that her pay was more like an allowance for a member of the family than the wages of a household servant, and that not only could she come and go any time she chose, but that all of her travel was a household expense. The very first thing she mentioned on the way from the post office and the main thing that everything we ever said or did always came back around to was school.

She said, I've been hearing a lot of very nice things about how fine you're still coming along over at the school, which was what most people who knew Mama and Papa and especially Miss Tee also used to say in one way or another. Sometimes all some of them used to do was call your name and nod and smile and give you the highball sign. I was used to that, and I also knew that you never could tell when somebody was also going to use it to try to hem you in with the same restrictions required of boys in training to become Catholic priests.

But as soon as she said what she said the way she said it, I crossed my fingers because I couldn't help wishing what I wished any more than anybody I ever saw in the barbershop or the bench on Stranahan's gallery could help shaking his head and sighing before straightening up and putting on his best manners whenever she came in sight.

So tell me about it, she said as we came on across that part of Buckshaw Mill Road and into the kite pasture, and I started with Miss Lexine Metcalf and by the time we opened her front gate I was talking about Mister B. Franklin Fisher, and we put the parcels down and sat on the front porch, me in the swing and her in one of the two cane-bottom rocking chairs, and that was when I told her about how when you were chosen to attend the Early Bird sessions that automatically put you in competition for a scholarship to college, and she said, Now that's something, now that's really something, and then she said, And aren't you something.

She said, I can't tell you how pleased I am about the way you're turning out. She said, I bet you didn't know that I was keeping tabs on you, and I said, I sure didn't, and she said, See there, you never can tell, and then she said, So from now on I am also going to be expecting to get some of my report directly from you in person. And with my fingers crossed again I said, If you say so.

Then she stood up and said, When do I get to hear something about your plans for yourself and I said, Anytime you say, and she said, Come on, let's go say hello to Mama, and I followed her around to the backyard and saw Miss Orita Bolden McGinnis who was also known as Miss Orita Bolden and Miss Reeta Mac. She was sitting on a wrought-iron bench under the scuppernong arbor, talking to Miss Sister Lucinda Wiggens and when she heard my name she looked up and held out her hand and said, Miss Melba's little old scootabout man, come on over here boy, just look at him growing on up to be a fine-mannered young gentlemen, and they tell me you got yourself a good head on your shoulders too. They tell me that that Miss what's-her-name Metcalf spotted his birthmark for learning the minute she set eyes on him. So you going give me a hug and some of that good old sugar like you used to, and I said, Oh yes, m'am.

Then Miss Sister Lucinda Wiggens opened her arms and folded me into her bosom and I had to give her some sugar on both cheeks and the lips too, and she said, Lord boy you precious, just precious. And she said, So many of our people don't care about nothing these days. Nothing but a lot of the same old foolishness. But some of us does care just like that Professor Fisher we got over yonder and you have our prayers to go right along with his strictness and all that book learning, and we all tells him to lay it on that precious few that got to make up for the many.

Back at the front gate I said, Next Tuesday would be just fine with me too. Then I could hardly wait to get somewhere and be all by myself. So when I came to the end of Gins Alley I didn't turn right and go directly home by way of the live oak shade cluster and the houses from which old Willie and Miss Meg Marlow moved to join Mister One Arm Will Marlow up in Detroit the year before Little Buddy Marshall came to town. I turned left into the old

pushcart and wheelbarrow lane between the tank-yard fence and
the skin-game thicket and came on down across the tank-car
sidings and along the L & N tracks and then back up through
cypress bottom to the chinaberry yard by way of Dodge Mill Road.

*When you came through the front door, the parlor was on your right and
the dining room was beyond the arch on your left and you saw yourself in
the big gilt-framed mirror above the long, low marble-top chest of drawers
against the back wall of the vestibule, and I also remember that there was
a telephone beside the mirror because it was the first one I ever saw in a
private home.*

*In the parlor there was a player piano with stacks of piano rolls lined
up across the top, and there was also a big console-model Victor victrola just
like the best one on display in the window of Jesse French Music Store on
Dauphine Street off the southwest corner of Bienville Square. As I remember
it, Jesse French was the biggest store in downtown Mobile for sheet music
and band instruments in those days, but what I always used to think about
whenever I heard that name was the black-spotted white dog figure sitting
on the pedestal out front with his ear cocked to hear his master's voice out
of the megaphone of a windup Victor victrola.*

*She left me on the settee which I guessed had been turned all the way
around from the fireplace because it was summertime, and you had a view
out through the double window and across the swing porch fern pots and
the rose bushes, and in the distance beyond the open plot between the house
across the street you could also see the sky above where you knew the Tensaw
River canebrakes bordered the route to Flomaton and Bay Minette and also
down into Pensacola and the Florida panhandle.*

*You could hear her moving about in the kitchen and also the sound
of spoons and ice clinking against glass, and then she was back with a
pitcher of lemonade and two glasses on a silver tray. She put it on the center
table and poured me a glassful and put a Chesterfield in her jeweled cigarette
holder, lit it with a kitchen match, and sat cross-legged in what I took to*

*be Miss Reeta Mac's rocking chair, laughing, one of the pink-bunny bedroom
mules on the tip of the toes of her left foot.*

*So tell me some more about yourself, she said then, and what I said
at first was still mostly about school because it was about all of the campus
sports activities I went out for such as football, basketball, and track and field
events and baseball to be sure which I also played off campus because I had
decided that I wanted to be a four-letter athlete as well as be an all-round
scholarship student, even though Mobile County Training School didn't
actually award MCTS sweaters because in those days the budget for
interscholastic extracurricular and recreational activities was barely
enough to cover the cost of basic regulation equipment and uniforms, even
when it was supplemented with the fund from the benefit drives and
programs that Mister B. Franklin Fisher was forever putting on to make
up the difference.*

*I said I could also play tennis, which was also mainly a campus game
in those days (as was volleyball which was only a recess time pastime at
Mobile County Training School when I was there). But you didn't have
time for tennis if you were as tied up with baseball as I had always been.
You didn't have to say anything about hunting and fishing because both
were just a natural part of living that close to the woods and swamps and
rivers and creeks. But I did mention swimming because I was the first one
in Gasoline Point to do the American crawl. Everybody else was still doing
the dog paddle, the sidestroke, the back paddle, and the fancy overhand until
I began showing some of them how much more speed you got when you kicked
and breathed like I had learned to do from a white boy named Dudy Tolliver
and also by watching the hundred-meter swimmers in the newsreels of the
Olympic games in Los Angeles.*

*We went on talking and that was when I found out that Miss Reeta
Mac was already across the bay visiting family people in Daphne and that
she herself was going over to join her the next day and also go down to Point
Clear and Magnolia Springs over the coming weekend, before heading back
to New York the following Wednesday night on the northbound L & N
Crescent Limited.*

That was when she began telling me the first part of what she was to tell me about herself over the next two years between then and the end of the summer after I got my diploma and my college scholarship and she gave me my going away present.

The very first thing she wanted me to know something about was what she did when she was away in New York and elsewhere, and she also explained just enough about her childhood across the bay for me to understand why she went to New York in the first place and then she told me about some of the things she guessed I wanted to know about what she liked about living in New York.

Then I heard the whistle of the three o'clock switch engine on the way from the L & N roundhouse across Three Mile Bridge to the tank-car sidings and realized how long I hadn't been there; but before I could decide what to say next, she said what she said, and I had to cross my fingers again.

Because as soon as she said, So now tell me something else, I was just about certain that I knew what was coming and sure enough, the very next thing she said was, What I want to find out about now is, how in the world did you manage to make it this far without getting trapped up in some of all this trouble down here in these bottoms. After all, she said, this is Gasoline Point. After all, this is jook joint junction.

She said, Unless I miss my guess, you know exactly what I am talking about and I said I did know and I did because I knew what had happened to Eddie Lee Sawyer and also to Tyner Beasley, not to mention Clarence Crawford, better known as Crawfish Crawford, all of whom were once Early Birds while I was still down in grade school. Eddie Lee Sawyer, who had dropped out of school in the tenth grade because he had to marry Mary Frances Henderson, was now the father of two girls and was driving a delivery truck for Hammels Department Store in downtown Mobile. Tyner Beasley had made it to the eleventh before he took up with Zelma Gibson and forgot all about becoming an architect and went to work as a handyman to keep enough money coming in to pay the rent with a little something left over for the honky-tonks.

As for Crawfish Crawford, who had been so brilliant in all of his mathematics and science classes, he had become so jealous of Miss Big Baby Doll Jackson who did you-know-what for a living that he had slit her throat from ear to ear and then had hidden out in the Hog Bayou for three months until they finally caught him on a tip from a moonshine runner and brought him to trial, and state solicitor Bart B. Chatterton had sent him to the penitentiary for ninety-nine years and a day.

She said, I sure do hope I'm right about you, because don't think I don't know what you been up to with all of them nice-boy manners and smiles and them sly twinkles in your eyes, and all I could say was that I hoped so too, and she said, I damn sure better be because after all, you're still just a minor in the eyes of the law, and then she also said, But God knows the truth of the matter is I just hope I didn't hold off until it's too late.

That was how we finally got to that part and all at once it was as if you had to keep touching the brake pedal because when she said, So well then, she was already standing up and as I followed down the hall it was suddenly as if what had happened back when Miss Evelyn Kirkwood said what she said that time was about something else altogether, because I was still only a boy then, and now I was almost a man.

But nobody could have made anything any easier than she was to do that first afternoon. She said, Now tell me one more thing. She said, You didn't give me any sugar the other day. You gave Mama some and you gave Miss Sister Lucinda Wiggens some. So how come you skipped me? And I said, Because they asked me and because you're different, and she said, Well can I have mine right here, right now? And as soon as I was that close she said, Well I declare well I just do declare, so I guess I must be different all right. It's a good thing this didn't happen out there in front of Mama. Then as I remember it, the next thing I heard was her saying, You can uncross your fingers now. You're doing fine, just fine.

When we said good-bye before she went back to New York at the end of that last summer before I was to leave for college, the graduation present she had saved to give me at that time was a Gladstone bag, and inside was the one-way ticket I needed to get me to the campus with my scholarship voucher. She said, So good luck, Miss Melba's Scooter, and when I said, Miss Slick McGinnis's Scooter, too, she said, That's just a little secret between you and me, and so is this little going-away present. Then she winked at me and I will always remember how her diamond ring finger felt as she squeezed my hands exactly like all of the other good fairy godmothers I ever dreamed about.

XVII

It is just about impossible to keep your thinking from becoming outright wishful when you are with somebody like Hortense Hightower, but I was not about to let myself jump to any hasty conclusions about what she was up to. I told myself that it was probably some sort of little game, that upper-level college man that I had finally become, I was supposed to be up to playing along with it until I found out whatever it was. In any case, the main thing was to keep from being faked into making a country break. Not that I was actually suspicious. There was no reason to feel that I was being set up. It really only was a matter of not taking for granted that somebody liked you on your own terms.

When I went back the week after that, she spotted me as soon as she came on, and at the end of the first set she came over and said, Say, there's my new schoolboy friend. What say, Schoolboy? Take care of my brand-new schoolboy friend, bartender. I was wonder-

ing when you'd come back to see me again. I was thinking about
how much I enjoyed talking to you.

So there she was, sitting on the next bar stool smiling at me
again, and it was not a matter of believing your luck or even of
what to say, because after she asked me about the campus routine,
she said, You know, when I was thinking about you I was also
thinking about how some people come in here all the time because
they just like to have some music going on around them when
they're sipping a little taste of something and jiving or maybe
conniving and carrying on.

Then she said, Now don't get me wrong. They all right with
me because that's all a part of what a place like this is here for, too.
Always has been. Some people just like to hear it without really
listening to it. But you can get to them because they feel it. Just like
they dance to it. That's how come when it stops, they stop whatever they're doing and start looking up and around like a fish in
a pond you just dried up.

But somebody like you, now, she said, now you're not just
hearing and feeling it. You also pay attention like you also got
something personal and private going on. Like me, she said, and I
don't mean like no musician either. Because I know a whole lot of
musicians can't hear doodly-squat. I know some can read anything
you put in front of them and then can't play anything you want to
hear, and I know some others that'll look at you like you crazy if
you want them to go back and read something they just played the
stew out of by ear. But later for all that, she said, because I can tell
you a few things about musicians. I know some that just come in
to watch you working so they can argue about what you did do or
didn't do, and you never know when they just looking for something to steal and sometimes when they can't find nothing they
want to steal they subject to say you ain't doing nothing. So later
for them. I don't call that listening to music because me, I'm just
up there trying to help people have a good time.

Which is exactly what she did when she came back on the floor show in which there was also a guest instrumentalist from Montgomery on alto sax whose solo feature was a takeoff of "Sweet Georgia Brown" which was very much like the one that Paul Bascombe was to record on tenor sax with Erskine Hawkins's band of mostly former 'Bama State collegians a year or so later.

I went back again that next Wednesday night and at one point in what was becoming our ongoing conversation, about listening and hearing, she said what she said about some hotshots from the campus who usually seemed to be mainly interested in showing how hip they were by making requests just to find out if she was up with the latest tunes they had been picking up on the radio and from the phonograph and that is how I found out that she herself still had every recording she had ever bought or had been given over the years.

So I said, What about Ma Rainey and Bessie and Clara and Mamie and Trixie? What about Jelly Roll and Papa Joe and Sidney Bechet and Freddie Keppard and young Satch and she just nodded, smiling, and said, Well, no wonder I noticed the way you listen. Because you listen like somebody already on some kind of real time. Because I can tell, and let me tell you something else. When you're already on some solid time you don't have to go around worrying about being up-to-date.

Then she said what she said about a college boy being the one who was supposed to know where stuff came from because that was also how you found out how and when it came to be the way it was as of now. That's what school is supposed to be all about, she said, and a hip cat ain't nothing but somebody trying to be a city slicker, and if you really think you can slick your way through life, shame on you.

Now that's what I say, she said, and that was also when she

told me that I was welcome to come by her house and play some of her records if I wanted to, and I said, I most certainly do want to, and when it was time to get ready for the next show, she described how to get to her neighborhood from the campus, and said what the best time was and left it at that.

So it was as if it was all up to me. But when she answered the doorbell that Sunday afternoon three days later and saw me standing there and said, So there you are, I could tell that she had actually been expecting me, and before I could apologize for intruding on her precious free time, she said, I'm sure glad you could make it. Come on in and let's get started.

So there I was indeed (with my wishes firmly in clutch and my senior year pretty much within reach and my long-range objectives a matter of no less urgency for being not yet specific), and there was the long living room with a nine-and-a-half-foot ceiling and there was the console-model Magnavox phonograph at the end where the floor-length draperies of the tall French windows were.

Some of the records, most of which were ten-inch and all of which were 78 rpm in those days, were in the built-in storage compartment, some were on the glass-top Hollywood coffee table between the overstuffed lounge chair and a hand-me-down rocking chair facing the console as if it were a fireplace, and there were others along with the stacks of sheet music on top of the white lacquer-finished grand piano near the arch where the Persian rug ended and the dining area which could be closed off with folding glass partition doors began.

I had never seen that many records of that kind anywhere before, and while I was looking through them and trying to make up my mind where to begin, she started the one that was already on the turntable, and as soon as I heard the first six notes of the piano intro I said, Hey, Earl Hines, hey Jimmy Mundy, hey "Cavernism," hey you, too, and she said, That's my favorite dance hall stomp-off and getaway number. Right after the theme, to break the ice and get 'em out there on the floor.

That's the one, she said when it was over, but now here's another one of it that they made about a year before that one and I like it too. I like those little differences in the call part of that opening phrase, she said, and I said, Me too, and I said, That guitar up front like that is all right with me too. Years later, Earl Hines was to tell me that he and Jimmy Mundy named that piece for a Washington, D.C., nightclub called the Cavern, but it was strictly Chicago music even so, because when you heard it going on the radio in those days, it was as if you were being taken to the South Side, just as Ellington's "Echoes of Harlem" took you to uptown Manhattan and Count Basie's "Moten Swing" took you out to Eighteenth and Vine in Kansas City.

The first side I handed her was old Jelly Roll Morton and the Red Hot Peppers playing "Kansas City Stomp" as if to charge the atmosphere of Gasoline Point with train whistles and sawmill whistles and riverboat and waterfront whistles. So that Little Buddy Marshall and I would have to do Old Luzana Cholly's sporty-limp strut going past dog-fennel meadows and crepe-myrtle yard blossoms en route once more to infield clay and outfield horizons by day and honky-tonk pianos by night.

I remember everything we played and hummed and whistled along with that first Sunday afternoon. After "Kansas City Stomp" I handed her Duke Ellington's "Birmingham Breakdown" which Little Buddy Marshall used to like to whistle and walk to as much as I did, especially when we were making the rounds beginning around twilight time on Saturday nights when the atmosphere of Gasoline Point was also charged with barbershop bay rum and talcum powder and the aroma of cigars, bootleg whiskey, and cookshop food.

And then one that Little Buddy and I also used to think of as our briar-patch music was Fletcher Henderson's orchestra playing "The Stampede." Then I said, Talking about something to make them so eager to get out there and cutting that they can hardly wait in the hat-check line, how about this? and I handed her "Big John's Special."

Then we went on to the one labeled "Wrapping It Up," but which coast-to-coast radio announcers call "The Lindy Glide" (as in lindy hop, another name for jitterbugging, as up-tempo dancing to jazz music was called in those days), and that led to "Back in Your Own Back Yard," "King Porter Stomp," "Stealing Apples," "Blue Lou," and "Sing You Sinners," which, like Bessie Smith's recording of "Moan You Mourners," was a mock church sermon pop song whose words I can still hear Nathaniel Tally, also known as Little Miss Nannie Goat of Tin Top Alley, shouting like stomping the blues with the Shelby Hill street-corner quartet backing him up, especially at a Saturday night fish- or chicken-plate benefit social.

Old Smack, she said, and started it again. Old Smack Henderson from right over there across the state line from Eufaula in Cuthbert, Georgia.

So we listened to it again right then, and we still had to hear it one more time as much as we both also liked "Wrapping It Up." When I realized to our surprise how quickly the time had passed and that I had to head back to the campus, and when I said what I said about the arrangement being strictly instrumental in spite of the fact that the lyrics for it were about singing, she said, That's Smack Henderson and when you got tenor players like Coleman Hawkins or Chu Berry or Ben Webster who is the one on this one, and you got trumpet players like Joe Smith, Red Allen, Rex Stewart, Roy Eldridge, and Emmett Berry who is the one on this and you got Buster Bailey and people like that, you ain't got much for a vocalist to do.

I don't mean he don't like them, she said. He knows what to do with them all right. Ethel Waters, Alberta Hunter, Bessie and Clara, Smith, Fletcher Henderson put some righteous stuff behind them and a whole lot of others. Then she said, But what about this? Here I am supposed to be a singer and this whole afternoon was strictly instrumental. But that's just the kind of singer I am, if you know what I mean. Ain't nothing like having all that good stuff behind you. I started out in the Mount Olive Choir and then went on to those bands. As far as I'm concerned, that's the getting place for my kind of singer. All them old pros sitting back there in them sections, and you got to go out every set and make them like having you up there. Now, that's the real conservatory for this stuff.

At the door she said, Wouldn't nobody believe that we didn't get around to but one thing by Duke Ellington, and not one bar of old Louis, and I said, I know I wouldn't and I was right here. Then when I said, I sure do thank you for letting me stop by like this, she said, Well now, you know your way over here and you got this many months left before graduation time.

XVIII

The main newspaper topic in the barbershop as I took my seat in front of Skeeter's chair that morning was baseball. There were only a few more weeks before opening day in the major leagues, and the preseason exhibition games were in full swing and just about all of the talk was about last year's World Series and this year's most likely pennant winners and how the stars in both leagues were shaping up and also about what outstanding rookie prospects were already beginning to show up.

Skeeter was touching up Red Gilmore who ran Red's Varsity Threads Shop next door and always came in on Tuesday, Thursday, and Saturday mornings to keep from looking as if he ever needed to go to the barbershop. Skeeter's chair was number two. In chair number one, Deke Whatley, the manager whose real name was Fred Douglass Whatley, was working on a sophomore basketball player known as Kokomo because that was the town in Indiana that he came from. The third chair was not in operation because

Thursday was Sack McBride's day off, and in the fourth chair Pop Collins was giving a facial to somebody I didn't know.

I did know who Pete Carmichael was. He was taxi number one and he was sitting on the high chair that Deke Whatley, who liked to keep his eyes on the shop and the sidewalk at the same time, used to rest his legs every now and then, but at the moment Pete Carmichael was sitting with his back to the window because he had the floor.

They went on talking about the spring training games of the big league baseball teams, and I heard them, but I was not really listening and following what points were being made because I was rereading the chapters on the commedia dell'arte, or comedy of improvisation of sixteenth-century Italy in a book entitled, *The Theatre: Three Thousand Years of Drama, Acting, and Stagecraft,* by Sheldon Cheney, and remembering how my roommate already knew so much about the masks, costumes, and characteristic gestures and stage business of such stock figures as Harlequin, Pantalone, Pierrot, Columbine, the pedantic Doctor, the swaggering but cowardly Il Capitano, when I mentioned the commedia dell'arte while we were talking about what we had been reading over the summer when he came back that second September. Later on we had also talked about how all of that was related to minstrels, medicine shows, and vaudeville skits, but now he was no longer around so that I could talk to him about what I was thinking about how it was also related to the way jazz musicians play and also to the way they work out their arrangements and compositions.

I was thinking about how whenever you talked to him about anything like that, you were in touch with somebody who was always ready to find out something else about customs, manners, and methods because as a student of architecture he was always involved with matters of design, construction, and engineers, and playing around with stage sets and puppet shows was as much a hobby with him as building and flying model airplanes and assembling and operating ham radios.

Then Skeeter had put the finishing touches on Red Gilmore, and it was my turn and I was sitting in the chair and being swung around toward the wall where all of the pictures, placards, and notices were and along with the chatter and laughter of the ongoing conversation, there was the also and also of clippers buzzing, scissors snipping, and also of shampoo and skin lotion and talcum powder and tobacco smoke, and outside there was the damp, overcast almost-spring weather, and you could also hear the droning and beeping traffic in that part of the morning on that part of the campus thoroughfare.

I looked at all of the long since familiar pictures of Jack Johnson and Peter Jackson and Joe Gans and Sam Langford and of Satchel Paige and Josh Gipson and Buck Leonard and Cool Papa Bell and of such entertainers as Bojangles Robinson and Charlie Chaplin and Bert Williams. Just when I came to the band leaders, I stopped and tried to shut everything out because I did not not want to start thinking about Hortense Hightower that early on in the day that I was going back to see her again, and when I opened my eyes and ears again, the talk was about politics and Deke Whatley had the floor.

He had a freshman in his chair then, and as usual he was working and talking with a short stump of a dead cigar in his mouth, his gold crowns showing as he clamped it in a way that reminded me of how some people hold a coffee cup or a drinking glass with that little finger extended, which is exactly what he did when he took the cigar out of his mouth from time to time.

Red Gilmore was sitting on the shoe-shine stand by the door that led to the back hallway and the toilet. He had the morning paper open and folded to a pad, working on a crossword puzzle as he waited for the bootblack to come in. The others sat listening to

Deke Whatley, who kept the clippers in his right hand all during the time that he was doing more talking than hair trimming. *Politics. Politics. Politics, he said. You want to know something about politics? I can tell you something about some goddamn politics. In the first place, it really don't take all that much. It really don't. It don't take a thing but some plain old horse sense mixed in with a little grade A bullshit, and of course you got to have some nerve, too, because how you going to bullshit if you ain't got no nerve. A good politician got the nerve of a brass-ass monkey.*

I can tell you something about some politics because I been watching that business for a long time. I been studying that business and watching what some somitches doing, so I'm talking about something I know from experience and mother wit. If you want to get somewhere in this man's world, you got to know how to play yourself some politics. That's a fact. Don't give a damn what nobody say. I'm telling you like it sure butt is as sure as you born. They supposed to be teaching them up yonder on the quadrangle, democracy and all of that no taxation without representation jive. You know what democracy is? I am going to tell you exactly what democracy is: playing politics. That's all it is. That's all it ever was and ever was intended to be and ever will be. Everybody playing politics. Everybody in there trying to get his little taste. You can say anything you want to, but you ain't never seen no somitch yet and you ain't never going to see one that wasn't out there for what he can get. Hell, ain't nobody going to admit it. Goddamn! old pardner, that's just what I'm telling about: horse sense.

He was into another one of his sermons then, as almost always happened when somebody said something academic about freedom and justice for all. He couldn't stand to hear anybody talk about the Constitution as if it were the Holy Bible. To him it was a document that was used for making deals and that was about all it was intended to be.

Ain't nobody but a fool or some old aristocrat going to be going around saying I'm all for me and to hell with you. You don't have to have no sense at all to know better than that. Hell, that other somitch is out there for hisself, too. And ain't no goddamn body going to think more of you than he do his own fucking self. Goddamn, gentlemen, and that's how come I know I don't really understand most of these old white folks to save my life. You see what I mean? You see what I'm driving at? Goddamn redneck somitch think they going to make you want to treat them better than you do your own precious goddamn self. Man, don't nobody come before me, not in my own heart and soul. You follow this stuff. That's something your goddamn dingdong is always telling you. That's all that somitch down there between your goddam legs ever know: me, me, me.

But now let me tell you something about them old aristocrats. When you come right down to it, that ain't nothing but the special few playing politics up there in the high society circles around the king. And don't care how bad-ass the king hisself is, he also got to be working some smooth jive to stay where he is and then if he really got his shit jumping, he can make hisself the goddamn emperor.

You see what I mean? And that's another thing we got to realize, too. I'm talking about us now. Ain't no mufkin white somitch going to give you nothing he don't have to. I'm talking about life now, cousin. This ain't no Sunday school out here. You got to get your ass out there and politic with them. Politic the hell out of them. You just find a way to get in there and dangle enough votes in front of one of them and he'll bring you your little taste, too. See if he don't. That's all it is. Everybody getting their little taste and that other fellow getting his little taste, too. That's what the king and them aristocrats forgot and that's how come so many of them wound up losing their hat, ass, and gas mask. You don't have to have no Ph.D. to dig that. Me, all I ever had was a little old country RFD myself, and I damn sure know it.

All right, now, you take Cat Rogers for instance. Take Cat Rogers right here in this county. You know why he can kick all them black asses and get away with it? Not so much because he so goddamn badass, although he is *as badass as almost any somitch I know. You got to admit that. Cat Rogers is one more badass peckerwood, gentlemen. I ain't joking. That's one out-and-out badass somitch on his own, starbadge or no starbadge. Don't let nobody fool you. That redneck somitch will pull off that goddamn badge and pistol in a minute just on general principles. You want to make it something personal? That's all right with him. But that ain't how come he can get away with it, because I know some badass boot somitches just as bad as he is, when you come right down to that. But he can get away with it and they can't because them that puts him in charge of the county jail lets him have his leeway, because it keeps things in line so they can keep their little taste coming like it always has. All this stuff is logic, gentlemen. You got to dig the logic of this stuff. Now get this. When these goddamn crybabies gang around talking about Cat Rogers this and Cat Rogers that, I tell them when you get yourself enough votes to get rid of Cat Rogers, you won't even have to get rid of him because he going to be seeing to it that you getting your little taste just like everybody else. Now that's politics, pardner, and that's what democracy is all about. Don't care what they got in them books up there.*

Then he said, Say boy, goddamn! Is your head shaped like this or is I'm cutting it like this? And everybody laughed and he stood back looking at the freshman's head as if he couldn't believe it was real.

Boy, you got the goddamndest head I ever seen in all my born days.

Everybody kept on laughing and the freshman was laughing, too. There was nothing wrong with his head and he knew it. Deke Whatley swung the chair around so that he could look out to the sidewalk and then he turned it so that the freshman could see himself in the mirror and then he want on talking in another tone of voice.

What's your name, son?

The freshman told him.

Where you from?

Birmingham.

You from the Ham?

Yes, sir.

What part of the Ham you from?

The freshman told him.

Goddamn, boy, you ought to *know* something if you come from the Ham. You know old Joe Ramey up in the 'ham?

Yes, sir.

Old Joe the Pro.

Yes, sir.

Boy, you know something. You supposed to know something. That goddamn Joe Ramey is the greatest cat in the world, boy. What'd you say your name was?

The freshman told him again.

Well, boy, if you know Joe Ramey, you know one hell of a cat. Hey, this boy is all right. Mark my words, gentlemen.

Hey, what the hell does this Joe Ramey do, Deke? Govan Edwards asked. He was not waiting his turn. He was there because the barbershop was one of the places he liked to drop in on several times a week. I knew him as a sports fan but I was never quite sure what he did for a living.

Do? Man, that goddamn Joe Ramey can do just about anything he want to. You know him, don't you, Red?

Who, Joe Ramey? Do I know Joe Ramey!

The door opened and Showboat Parker, cab number nine, the only Cadillac taxi in town, stuck his head in and said, Hey, in here, and came on in pushing the door shut behind him and leaning back against it as he checked to see who all was present.

I said, Hey in here, he said, and somebody said, Shoby, and somebody else said, What say Shoby, and somebody else said, What's happening Shoby, and he said, Man, ain't nothing happening, and this is the weather for it. What's the matter with these people? and somebody said, The day is still young, give them time, Shoby. But you must have picked up some kind of news out there.

Man, ain't no news, he said. White folks still out in front that's all I can tell you. And when Pete Carmichael said, Well that sure God ain't no news, he said, You goddamn right it ain't. Us white folks so far ahead of you cotton-picking granny dodgers, it ain't even funny no more. And when Pop Collins said, Hell, it ain't never been funny, he said, Hell, it better not be funny. What the fuck, you'd think this is. This ain't no goddamn vaudeville. This is life in the nitty goddamn gritty. You goddamn people always laughing too much anyhow.

Hey, wait a minute now, Deke Whatley said, holding up his clippers, Hey now hold on there because that ain't the way I heard it. The way my grandpappy told me, all that grinning and laughing is a part of our African mother wit, because the first thing our African forefathers found out after they realized that all them hungry-looking peckerwoods was not going to eat them was that if you didn't grin at them, white folks would be scared shitless of us all the goddamn time and ain't no telling what they might do. My old grandpa told me, if you ain't got nothing but a stick and a brick, you don't go around making somebody nervous that's got cannon and a Gatling gun.

Then he said, But now tell me this. If white folks so far out in front, how come they spend so much time worrying about what we doing? They supposed to have everything already nailed up and they always coming up with another one of these books to prove that we too dumb to figure out how to get it unnailed.

You got me the answer for that? he said, and Showboat Parker said, Now come on, Deacon, you know good and well that us white folks don't have to account to the likes of y'all for nothing we do. It ain't for y'all to understand how come us white folks doing anything. We just want y'all to learn how to read well enough to know your place, and we got a million-dollar school right here to teach you.

They were all laughing again then, and he said, What say there, Red Boy? What say, Skeets and the rest of y'all?

Skeeter swirled the chair, and you could see them in the

mirror. Showboat sat in Sack McBride's empty chair and leaned back, crossing his legs and folding his hands over his taxi driver's paunch, his cap tipped down over his eyes.

Where were you last night, Red Boy?

Trying to get somewhere and do myself some good, man, Red Gilmore told him.

The boys missed you.

Man, I couldn't make it. Not from where I was last night.

The stuff was there.

How'd you make out?

Man, me, I ain't held a decent hand yet.

What about Old Saul?

Aw, man, they cleaned Old Saul Baker out way before midnight. Man, Old Saul was probably home in bed by midnight last night.

How about Giles?

Man, don't say nothing to me about no Giles Cunningham.

Old Giles, hunh?

That goddamn Giles Cunningham is one of the gamblingess somitches in the world today.

Old Giles checked them to the locks, hunh?

I believe that somitch would have broke the Federal Reserve last night, man.

Old Giles.

Talking about hot, goddamn but that somitch was hot last night.

Yancey got them tonight?

Yeah.

That's what I thought. I guess I might peep me a few of them myself this evening.

You welcome to it, Red. But me, man, the hell with some old poker tonight. Man, I know something else I can do with my little change beside giving it to that goddamn Giles Cunningham.

148

When I left, they were still talking about Giles Cunningham, but on the way back to the dormitory I was thinking about Old Dewitt Dawkins once more because he was the one that listening to Deke Whatley always made me remember again. Old Dewitt Dawkins who had the best reputation of any baseball umpire and prizefight referee anywhere in the Mobile and Gulf Coast area.

Old Dewitt Dawkins, also known as Judge Dawk the Hawk because when he used to come into Shade's Tonsorial Parlor across from Boom Men's Union Hall on Greens Avenue (always with the latest editions of the Reach and Spalding baseball guides and his up-to-date world's almanac), it was very much as if the circuit judge had come to town to hold court and deliver verdicts, which he did with lip-smacking precision in a diction that was deliberately stilted.

The first thing that probably came to most people's minds when you mentioned Dewitt Dawkins was the way he used to call baseball games back in those days before the radio sportscasters became the voice you associated with the ongoing action. There was a time when all of the baseball youngsters in Gasoline Point used to say *In the window!* for a called strike because that was the way Dawk the Hawk (as in hawkeye) called them.

But what the political gospel according to Deke Whatley had brought back to my mind was something that I had heard from Old Dewitt Dawkins in his high seat on the shoe-shine stand in Shade's barbershop one rainy afternoon in August of the summer before my junior year at Mobile County Training School when he was explaining why we already had too many people signifying and not nearly enough qualifying.

Not that he wasn't still calling balls and strikes. No matter what he was talking about, he spread his hands to give the safe-on-base sign when he agreed with or approved of something. When somebody made a point or he himself was giving the word, he gave the strike sign to indicate it was on target, which was to say *In the window!* So to show his disagreement or disapproval, he jerked his thumb giving the *out* sign to which he would sometimes add with his most stiltedly precise enunciation:

> Tough
> shit (pause)
> you done torn
> your
> na-
> tu-
> ral-
> ass!

Out of my face, out of my face. Out of my face, you disgrace to the human race.

What the hell do we need with some more loudmouth hustlers out there carrying on like they got to get those people told because nobody ever did before, he said that afternoon.

That many of us were all in Shade's because the game with Maysville had been called for weather in the second inning. Hell, as far as that goes, we already had a silver-tongue orator none other than the one and only Honorable Fred Douglass himself doing that all the way back during bondage and on into the war for Emancipation and right on through the whole Reconstruction mess and into the times of old Grover Cleveland, and I don't know anybody that ever did it better since.

He said, We don't need any more horror stories trying to put the shame on those people as if they don't know what the hell they themselves been doing to us all these years. Just look at what they did to *Uncle Tom's Cabin*. Those same people put on black faces and turned the whole goddamn thing into a big road-show minstrel, traveling all over the country.

So much for getting them told, he said, and then he said, Now I'm going to tell you something once and for all about the shame and the blame. If you got the problem and don't buckle down and come up with a solution, hang your own goddamn head in shame, and if you go all the way through college and don't come back with some answers, shame on us all.

XIX

What happened between Giles Cunningham and Dudley Philpot out at the Pit while I was browsing in the periodicals room later on that afternoon had really begun almost a week earlier when Giles Cunningham and Wiley Peyton had stopped Will Spradley as he came along the railroad spur that used to run from the loading ramp and coal chute at the campus power plant and on through town and out to the siding at the station where trains eastbound from Montgomery and westbound from Atlanta used to stop without being flagged in those days.

It was payday for most people who didn't work on the campus, and before leaving on a three-day business trip up to Chattanooga, Giles Cunningham was making the rounds to collect a few overdue personal loans he had made during the past several months. When he and Wiley Peyton saw Will Spradley, they were on their way to see who just happened to be hanging out in Jack's Chicken Shack just outside the campus entrance near the band cottage.

Will Spradley had been just rounding the bend near the old Strickland mansion and had been coming on walking that loping walk toward where the first downtown subdivision began, when Wiley Peyton who was driving saw him and said, Well, here's your Will what's-his-name over there, and Giles Cunningham had said, Pull over, and Wiley Peyton had brought the big Cadillac onto the soft shoulder and shut off the motor, and Giles Cunningham had said, Spradley, Will; and Will Spradley had jumped and said, Gile, what say, Gile? and came down the grade and across the grassy ditch and up to the car and said, Gile, again. What say, Gile?

Will Spradley had stood looking into the car but at the dashboard, not at Giles Cunningham who was not looking at him either but at the misty early spring tree-line beyond the fence on the other side of the spur tracks and who said, Don't you have a little something to see me about? and Will Spradley had said, Yeah, Gile, sure Gile, I ain't forgot it, Gile.

I was just going on down into town and I was coming right on by to see you just as soon as I took care of some other little business first, Will Spradley had said then, talking and then listening, but still not looking at anything but the dashboard, and when there was no reply he had gone on and said, That's exactly what I was on my way to do, Gile.

Then Giles Cunningham had said, So here I am just tickled to death to save you that long walk. He still didn't look at him but he was listening very carefully because he knew that with Will Spradley you almost always had to read between the lines.

I'm going to have to see you a little later, Gile.

Today's payday, ain't it?

I mean later on today, Gile. I'm talking about today, a little later on today, Gile.

You been paid, ain't you?

I'm going to see you later on, Gile. I'm going to have your money then, every penny I been owing you, Gile.

You mean, you ain't got it on you? I thought you just said you already been paid.

I mean, I just want you to let me see you a little later on, Gile. That's all I mean. I just mean I can't pay you right now, he said, and Giles Cunningham said, Now what kind of shit is this, man? You got your paycheck, didn't you, or is that it?

Wiley Peyton sat at the steering wheel looking along the corridor of the March green branches of the wooded bend on the left side of which you could see the turnoff that led to the stone pillars and wrought-iron gates to the old Strickland manor house. The strip of off-campus shops, including Jack's Chicken Shack, was out of sight about a quarter of a mile farther along, and then there was the campus.

He heard what was being said and not being said, and it was all old stuff to him, and besides it was not really anything that concerned him. What he spent most of his time dealing with was the operation of the Pit. But even so he heard Will Spradley say that he had the check with him, and he knew what was coming next.

Aw, hell, man, I thought you were talking about some kind of a problem.

So I'm going to see you later on, Gile.

You already got your check, so see me now.

But it ain't cashed yet, Gile. That's how come I got to be getting on downtown just now.

Man, what the hell you talking about? The goddamn bank been closed for nearly two hours.

But that's not what I'm talking about, Gile. I got some other little business I got to see to first. Then I going to be right on out there to see you.

Where you going to see me?

At your place.

Which place?

Which one you going to be at?

I'm on my way out of town.

Well, when you get back then.

The hell you will. Here, I'll cash your check. He stretched his legs, pushing his shoulders against the back of the seat and pulled a roll of bills out and took a fountain pen and a flat check-holder from his inside coat pocket.

Hey, you can't do that, Gile.

Can't do what, man?

You can't cash it.

Man, you wasting my time. Sign that goddamn check and hand it here.

Will Spradley didn't move. He was looking at both of them then, but Wiley Peyton was still looking straight ahead, and Giles Cunningham just sat waiting and listening as if not looking at anything in particular, but he saw Will Spradley take a step back from the car as he heard him say, I can't do it, Gile. I done told you I'm going to pay you what I owe you and I will, but I owe somebody else and he supposed to cash my check.

Man, what's the difference who cashes it? Now you going to sign that fucking check and hand it here, or do I have to get out of this car and kick your ass? Man, I don't feel like kicking nobody's ass today. I just want my little change so I can be on my way. Look, I'm even going to forget about the goddamn interest. Here, just sign the son-of-a-bitch and get the hell out of my face.

Aw right, Gile, Will Spradley said then. But I'm telling you, man. I'm talking about Dud Philpot.

So when Giles Cunningham looked out from where he was sitting at the desk in the office he shared with Wiley Peyton at the Pit and saw the dull gray Plymouth come crunching onto the gravel drive-way and saw Dudley Philpot hop out, not even pausing to slam the door, and come fuming into the dining room, he was not surprised because Will Spradley had already been there with a message from him.

Through the door to the dining area you could see several people sitting on stools eating at the counter and there were several more at a table near the jukebox. Wiley Peyton sat at the cash register because it was that part of the late afternoon when business was always very light and someone had to relieve the regular cashier so that she could always have three hours off before the dinner rush began.

Without really looking up from what he was doing, Giles Cunningham could see Dud Philpot go over to Wiley Peyton, and Wiley Peyton pointing him toward the office and then there he was, just standing with his hands on his hips, trying to look his white boss-man look but also trying to get his breath back without seeming to, and at first Giles Cunningham went on doing what he was doing and then he looked up as if he had just seen him. But he didn't say anything.

Wasn't Will Spradley in here?

I was under the impression that he left out of here some time ago, but I don't know which way he went.

Well, didn't he tell you what I said?

He didn't say nothing that made any sense at all to me, and I didn't have time to be bothered with him today anyway.

You didn't have time to be bothered with Will Spradley? It was me that sent Will Spradley in here. Me.

Well, what he said didn't make no sense.

He was standing up then, and he picked up some papers and moved over to the filing cabinet by the window, dropped them into the wire basket on top and stood for a moment, not as if he were listening and waiting, but as if trying to decide what office routine detail had to be taken care of next.

So what the hell you think I came all the way out here for?

I figured you were trying to catch up with Will Spradley and I told you he ain't out here. He was in here all right, but that was a while ago.

I came out here to see you, Giles Cunningham, and you damn well know it, and you damn well know why, so cut out the horseshit.

Man, I sure must have missed something somewhere along the line, because I sure in hell can't remember ever having any dealings with you in my life. So I don't know what you talking about.

I'm talking about that check.

Well, there sure ain't nothing I can do about that because I already deposited it. I told Will Spradley that and I thought for sure that he had told you by now.

Now listen here, Giles Cunningham, Will tells me he begged you not to cash that check in the first place. Is that right?

It sure is. He didn't tell you no lie about that.

And that's what you got to answer to me for.

Man, you can't be saying that Will Spradley told you something to make you believe I took more out of that check than I had coming to me. I don't know what he did with the rest of his cash after he left me, but he sure in the hell can't blame it on me. Hell, I didn't even take out all I had coming.

But he knew very well that nobody was accusing him of any such thing. He was cross-talking Dudley Philpot and they both knew it because they both also knew what very old and very grim down-home game Dudley Philpot was turning the matter of Will Spradley's paycheck into, although Dudley Philpot would never have called it a game, because to him games were something you played for fun and what he had on his hands was the very urgent obligation to keep things in proper order.

But to Giles Cunningham it was no less a game for being as serious and dangerous as it was. The very way that Dudley Philpot was standing there just inside the door with his hands on his hips was an unmistakable part of the game, and so was the way he himself was pretending not to notice how much more upset Dudley Philpot was becoming.

Outside the window there was the highway of black rubbery-looking asphalt in the afternoon mist, with the cars and trucks splitting by, buzzing and rumbling as if in a passing parade in a newsreel world apart, and he remembered the trip back from Chattanooga in the rain and wondered when he was going to find time to have that Tennessee and northern Alabama red-clay hillbilly mud washed off his white sidewalls.

Then he realized that Dudley Philpot was swearing at him and he was not surprised because that was a part of the game, too, but at first it was as if all Dudley Philpot was saying was nigger nigger nigger nigger nigger nigger, and that didn't surprise him either, and then what he heard was answer me nigger answer me answer me and he said, I don't answer to no name like that.

You could tell that Dudley Philpot didn't really know what to do next, because then he just stood there clenching his fists and fuming and saying nigger nigger nigger, you nigger you nigger nigger nigger, you nigger, you nigger. Nigger! Then all at once it was as if he realized that he was acting and sounding like a daddy fyce puppy dog in a small-town neighborhood running along inside the fence line yap-yap-yapping at a passerby who was annoyed and alert but was also trying to keep himself from busting out laughing. So that's when he said what he said next.

Nigger, I'm beginning to get the notion that you think you smart or something, but meddling in my business is getting too smart. And when all Giles Cunningham did was just shrug his shoulders at that, he said, Nigger I got a good mind to kick your black ass till your nose bleeds shit right here and now.

But he didn't move from where he was, so Giles Cunningham didn't have to say I know you know better than that. Even so, he couldn't keep

*himself from giving him his old AEF fixed bayonets eyeball to eyeball
you-got-to-bring-ass-to-kick-ass look, and that was more than enough.*

*All right, you uppity black son-of-a-bitch, you're lucky. You don't
know how lucky you are. I'm going to give you one night to get your black
ass out of this county, and I don't want to ever set eyes on you again. You
got that?*

*He said that screaming at the top of his voice so that everybody out
in the cafe and also back in the kitchen could hear him, and then those in
the cafe saw him stomping out, glaring at nothing in particular, and saw
him hop back into the Plymouth and slam the door. Then they heard the
motor stall and start and stall and then start and hold and saw him throw
it into reverse and cut the front end around as if he were riding a saddle
horse and head back toward town.*

XX

When I came out of the library on my way to the dining hall through the late March twilight of that damp, green Thursday evening, I was thinking about my freshman and sophomore year roommate again who would have gone into his old mock penny-dreadful palm-rubbing and mustache-twirling heh-heh-hey routine as soon as he looked up and saw how many books on the commedia dell'arte I had just checked out.

Then he would have reached for his pad of 8½″ × 11″ grid paper and sketched several examples of the makeshift all-purpose stage platforms that the old traveling troupes of actors, musicians, and jugglers used to set up on the streets and in the squares of town after town back in sixteenth-century Italy and France, and you had to make the connection with minstrels, medicine shows, and vaudeville acts, after which he would come up with some fact about the famous drawings and sketches of Jacques Callot that you had either missed or hadn't yet come across.

And then for the next several days you could count on him

taking time out from his own current works-in-progress to play around, dashing off sketches and watercolor illustrations and maybe even a few woodcuts of masks, costumes for most of the stock characters and standard scenarios, beginning with Harlequin (wearing diamond patterns based on Picasso's blue and rose period Harlequin), Brighella (who was as foxy as Reynaud), and including old Pantalone, Il Dottore, Il Capitano, Pulcinella, Scaramouche, and so on to Columbine and Pierrot (which he would make sure that you knew was the French version of the Italian Pedrolino or Pierotto).

Nor would he be able to stop here. The next step would be a desktop stage model or a puppet show for which we would have to improvise our own skits for a week or so just as an exercise for the two of us, and only the two of us, because if you as much as even mentioned it to anybody else you would be accused of trying to impress them. As if you didn't know better than that. Anyway, the only part of it that anybody else would see would probably be two or three leftover sketches or watercolors that he would have tacked up on his side of the room where they would be mistaken for examples of class exercises in design.

That was the way he always was about things like that, and that is the way I knew it would have been if he had still been there, and it was also why he was not somebody you tried to compete with. He was somebody to try to keep up with to be sure, but not because you didn't want to be left behind, outstripped, but because it was as if he were there to keep you reminded of what Miss Lexine Metcalf's windows on the world bulletin board was really all about.

But he was no longer there on that early spring evening, because he had decided to take the Old Trooper up on his option and had transferred to an Ivy League college for his junior and senior years.

That was the very first thing he told me as soon as he came back from Chicago that second September. But it was not until that following spring that he finally got around to saying what he said about the farewell caper he owed it to himself to pull off a few times before cutting out for good.

The main thing he wanted to talk about as he sat unpacking as a sophomore was what had happened during the summer, especially the trip he had made with the Old Trooper that July. The two of them had driven from Chicago to New York, stopping long enough in Cleveland, Pittsburgh, and Philadelphia to visit the art museums as well as the architectural and engineering landmarks he had wanted to find. In New York he had been given free time on his own to spend in the Metropolitan Museum, the Museum of Modern Art, and the Museum of Natural History and had also made the rounds with the Old Trooper to see the Yankees in Yankee Stadium, the Giants at the Polo Grounds, and the Brooklyn Dodgers at Ebbets Field, and naturally went along to watch the boxers working out in Stillman's Gym and to Madison Square Garden which was on Eighth Avenue between Forty-ninth and Fiftieth Streets in those days.

What he was mainly curious to know about my summer on the campus as a working student was how much reading I had gotten in, and when I told him that along with everything else I had checked off my list I had made it all the way through both volumes of Charles and Mary Beard's *The Rise of American Civilization,* he wanted to know if I had also looked into Beard's *Economic Interpretation of the Constitution,* and he also asked about Thorstein Veblen's *Theory of the Leisure Class* and *Theory of Business Enterprise,* and Frederick Jackson Turner's *The Frontier in American History,* and that was what led to all of the reading and talking about social contracts and political structures and procedures (including socialism and fascism) during the months that followed.

When he saw that I had also checked out the new editions of

Louis Untermeyer's *Modern American Poetry* and *Modern British Poetry* on extended loans, he said I also had to get *Axel's Castle* by Edmund Wilson and *Exile's Return* by Malcolm Cowley, which I did as soon as the library opened the next day, and that was what got me going on James Joyce and Marcel Proust (but not Hemingway whom I had already discovered in *Scribner's* magazine and the first issues of *Esquire* magazine back at Mobile County Training School), and not Faulkner who was already there along with and head and shoulders above such other Southern writers as T. S. Stribling, Erskine Caldwell, and Margaret Mitchell whose *Gone With the Wind* had been a best-seller for about a year.

As for his own summer reading, he had knocked off about his usual quota of detective stories featuring Hercule Poirot, Bulldog Drummond, Ellery Queen, Sam Spade, and Nero Wolfe, and he had also read John Steinbeck's *Tortilla Flat*, and Kenneth Roberts's *Northwest Passage*. But the two books he had stuck with all summer and had taken along on the trip east were Sheldon Cheney's *Primer of Modern Art* and Roger Fry's *Vision and Design*, and what he had read on the train coming down this time was *Man's Fate* by André Malraux, so his first two checkouts from the library were going to be *The Conquerors* and *The Royal Way*.

He didn't mention anything at all about any kind of special farewell caper until it was wisteria time again that next spring and he was ready to get started on it, and at first I missed the point and said what I said about Floorboard McKenzie, who was the local limousine with the best connections across the line in those days, and that was when he spelled it out, saying that he wasn't dismissing anybody for using Floorboard because that way was no less a matter of life and death in his neck of the woods.

But what he had in mind for his own personal derring-do response to that particular down-home taboo was something else, and he said, Don't let anybody tell you that the one in question whoever she may be is not worth risking your life for, because the woman is not what really counts. It's the taboo. Because once they put that life and death price on the taboo that makes them all worth it, because they have to feel as violated and outraged when it is a cathouse slut as when it is Miss All-City Belle.

So there is no way around it for us either, he said. If you're one of us, you have to commit a deliberate violation of that particular taboo before you can really call yourself a man. No matter what else you ever do, that's something you have to answer to yourself for, and you're either game or you're not, he said; and then he also said, Hey, but maybe all of this is all knee-high-to-a-duck stuff to you, and I said, Not really because I had never thought about it as being a matter of the kind of taboo and derring-do he was talking about.

What Mama had always been saying about keeping out of trouble with girls and about not letting friendly white ones grin your neck into a noose was as much a part of my conception of the everyday facts of life in Gasoline Point as everything else I was always being warned about. But the way Trudie Tolliver said what she finally said that day when I met her coming along Dodge Mill Road from the landing where the skiffs and putt-putts tied up in Three Mill Bottom made the actual here-and-nowness of it sound like something you had to be very, very careful about, to be sure, but not at all like anything that you always had to avoid by all means. After all, doing something like that was always supposed to be a matter of privacy if not secrecy whoever the female partner was.

So the main thing I remember about how I felt about that first time with Trudie Tolliver with her storybook blue eyes and cornsilk golden lashes, lip fuzz, and dog-fennel meadow and her piney woods voice and sweet gum twig breath and tomboy toes is how lucky I was being let in on one more secret, and with Miss Evelyn Kirkwood I remember feeling even luckier because I was still only an early-teen boy then and she was thirty something, maybe going on forty.

At first I had just thought that Trudie Tolliver was a girl who wanted to go everywhere her brother went, so she was always around whenever she could be only because Dudie Tolliver (as in Dude) was the one who used to take me duck hunting and boat fishing and trout-line setting and also swimming and bridge diving, beginning shortly after his family moved into the back of the Last Chance store his father was managing at the end of Old Buckshaw Mill Road and U.S. 90 near the new drawbridge, and he kept it up until his father got a job managing another store and moved on into Mobile.

It was from Duane Dundee, better known as Dude and Old Dudie, Tolliver that I learned to do the American crawl that the Tarzan movies and the newsreels of the Olympics were to make so much more popular than the fancy overhand stroke and scissors kick a few years later, and he also taught me a lot of other things that I was to continue to find out more about by reading Field and Stream *magazine later on. So until that afternoon, as friendly as she always was, she was only somebody you had to put up with unless her brother could convince her that it was not one of the times she could come along.*

But that afternoon in the bottom, it was as if she and I had been very close friends all along and I knew that she was going to start teasing me even before she said what she said. She said, I bet you wish you knew the secret I know, and when I said, Why, she said, Because it's about you, and I said, How you going to know if it's true if you don't tell me so I can tell if it's so, and she said, Because I saw it all for myself, and I said, That's what you say but it doesn't count if I don't know what it is because anybody can just come up and say something like that. So she said, Well maybe I will if you promise not to tell Dudie, and I knew I didn't have to, because all you had to do was look at how her eyes were mocking you and there was no doubt that she couldn't wait to tell you anyway. But I did promise, and she said, I saw your trigger, and I said, My what? as if I didn't know and she said, I spied on you and Dudie swimming naked down there around the bend from One Mile Bridge. And I tried to get my hand in my pocket, and she said, I see you, Scooterboy, so now you want to root me right this minute and you know it and I know it. And I couldn't deny it because I couldn't even take my hand back out of my pocket.

She said, Keep on going until you get all the way around the curve then turn on around and come on back halfway up the hill and turn off to the trail to the right, and this is my signal, and she whistled one of the bird songs that old Dudie had probably already taught her before they came to Gasoline Point and he started teaching me.

There was a different bird-song signal for every time between that summer afternoon in the L & N thickets and twilight of the last autumn night before her family moved on into the city limits of Mobile. As for the risk I was running for that many months, it was as if once it all got started all of Mama's terrifying warnings about a gang of rednecks tying you up and shucking your life seeds like two raw oysters no longer applied to you if you were always careful enough. You didn't even have to mention anything at all about that part of it, and the closest we ever came to doing so was the time she said what she said about having something on old Dudie because she knew that he gave something from the store to a certain notorious dark brown-skin Gasoline Point party to get her to go into the bushes with him, and then she said, He ain't got nothing on me and he not going to get nothing. Unless you tell him, she said.

With Miss Evelyn Kirkwood it was almost as if you were not really taking very much of a chance at all, because all you had to do was what she said because she was a grown-up and I was only in my early teens, and every time I was in her presence during the four or five weeks that we were doing what we did I was supposed to be running routine errands and then helping her to get packed to join her husband up in Muscle Shoals near the Tennessee state line where he had moved on to a new civil engineering project when he finished his contract on the Alabama State docks along Mobile River. But I was not really working for her because as hard as Papa always had to hustle to make ends meet, he and Mama were dead set against ever hiring me out to white folks. So as far as they were concerned, I was over there as a return favor for something Mister Garrett Kirkwood had done for Papa.

She said, You smell like you just washed yourself with Pine Tar soap. That's nice. That's Aunt Melba and Uncle Whit and all that sweeping and brushing and scrubbing and washing for you. So come on in and come on over here and let me look at you. Nice. Very nice. Don't be afraid. You're not afraid of me, are you? I always thought that you thought that I was a very pretty lady, she said, and I said, I do. Because she was, with what I now remember as her Gainsborough eyes and complexion and her anatomy-sketchbook calves and insteps. I'm not going to bite you, she said. That's a good boy, she said. Nice, very nice. You knew I wasn't going to bite you, didn't you, she said. Because it sure doesn't look to me like you're scared one bit. So I guess I must know something about picking and choosing brown sugar lumps, she said. And she did not say anything at all about not telling anybody because she knew she didn't have to; but she did emphatically say, And don't be calling me no Miss Eve like in evil. Call me Miss Ev. Everybody else called her Miss Evelyn or Miss Evelyn Hughes (as in the old Hughes family and place up the Tombigbee) or Miss Evelyn Hughes Kirkwood, and so did I when something about her came up in public, but in private she sometimes gave me other names to call her along with some of the things she told me to do.

You know something, man, I told my roommate, man, that's just not something you let yourself go around thinking about. I said, Man, once you get away with some stuff like that you're glad it happened, and that's it.

As for the caper that he had decided that he owed it to his conception of himself to try to bring off before ending his sojourn in the Deep South, he had already spotted somebody who met all of his requirements. She was a certified Southern belle from a bona fide antebellum mansion who just happened to be a co-manager of a department store on Courthouse Square a few doors down from Tate and Davidson's, not because she had been trained for a career in the retail business but because she had inherited half-ownership from a childless uncle on her mother's side of the family.

Do you know the one I'm talking about, he said, and I said, No but I'll take your word for it, and he said, Not this time, old pardner, because sophomores that we still are alas I want to make sure that you don't jump to any sophomoric conclusions about wishful thinking, compensation, or some other Viennese bullshit. He said, I want you to go down there and see for yourself, old pardner, I insist, old pardner. So I did go down as if looking around for a gift for a girlfriend, and when I saw her come out of the office I caught my breath and crossed my fingers, and when I finally came back to the room from the gym that night I said, Man I sure am still a sophomore all right because I do believe you wished it all up and sent me down there knowing that I would see only what you wanted me to see, and he said, No Pygmalion I and no Galatea she. So I said, That leaves us with Herr Doktor Faustus and his snake-oil princess, and he said, Some snake some oil some princess.

She may have been a year or two older than we were, but she had been away to finishing school and on cruises to Europe and the Near East, and perhaps that along with her several years of very active experience as a businesswoman made her seem older than she was and certainly older than she looked, which was less than twenty-five at most.

Whatever her exact age, she was the kind of very good-looking and casually style-conscious young Southern woman that images of certain New York fashion models have been based on for generations. Also, not only was she herself one of the most prominent young women in town and not only was her store as popular as it was classy, but it also had the most up-to-date college shop in town, which attracted a lot of students from the campus in spite of all of their very strong reservations about shopping in a store facing a courthouse square with a Confederate army memorial as its centerpiece.

So the first step turned out to be easy. He went into the manager's office and introduced himself as a student of architecture and design who wanted to ask her some questions about current trends in fashion, art, and interior decoration for a term project he was working on, and before he came back out he had also made her aware of his easy and thorough familiarity with every type of article in the current and recent issues of Vogue, Harper's Bazaar, Vanity Fair, *and* House and Garden *stacked on her desk.*

Within the next ten days, he was being paged to take phone calls in the booth off the lounge, at first just about every other night, and then every night, and within the month she had begun picking him up either in her sedan or her coupé, sometimes in the traffic circle between the gym and the tennis courts, sometimes near the water tower near the science hall and sometimes in the parking lot behind the library, and they would drive out to one of the campus groves or orchards that were a part of the horizon you saw when you looked out across the fields and pastures from the administration center of the school of agriculture.

Then suddenly after the third rendezvous the whole thing became a very private matter that he hardly ever mentioned except in passing until the final week of his last spring term when he started packing his luggage to pull out for good in the next day or so. I knew he was going to bring it up then, and he did. He said, About my caper I know you would understand what was happening. At first it was something I had to do for the hell of it but as soon as it actually became something person to person, it was no longer my caper but also her caper and so our caper, so from then on the taboo was as much a catalytic agent as it was anything else. If you know what I mean, he said, and I said, I think I do, I really do. But when I said what I said about answers to the old folks' prayers, there was an unmistakable touch of tolerant surprise and exasperation in his old playful sidewise glance and conspiratorial wink and smile as he said, That rather depends on which old folks one's been listening to, doesn't it old pardner? What about the ones who say you can never really call yourself a man among men until you have taken it on yourself to pull the caper I tried and get away with it. Come on man, I thought we agreed that we do indeed choose some of our ancestors.

But don't get me wrong about this caper thing, roommate, and don't play yourself cheap because I'm not. I wouldn't lie to you, old pardner. And he said, You know something? As pleased as I can't help but be about how all of this turned out I still find myself wishing that she had been the one who picked me out. So don't think I don't know that down-home boys who've been through what you've been through don't feel that they have to go through what I took on. I know as well as you do that it can't possibly add up to the same results.

So what now? I said as he went on packing his steamer trunk. And he said, The moving finger having writ moves on. It turns out that she does get up to Chicago on business trips from time to time, and she might give me a call as she volunteered to do. Or she might not. Meanwhile it was what it was and I'm better off for it.

Then three days later, his sojourn in the central Alabama strip of the briar patch at an end, he had cut back out to Chicago once more from where he was to move on to the also and also of other temporary destinations, beyond which there would always be still other horizons evoking newly pertinent ancestral aspirations and expectations and therefore obligations accepted or not, fulfilled or not.

Nor did any of that seem to faze him very much, if at all. Not him who was forever reminding me as well as himself that for all your carefully laid plans and expert training and guidance, a picaresque story line was the perpetual frame of reference for all personal chronicles.

Not T. Jerome Jefferson, T for Thomas, J for Jerome as in Geronimo, Apache or not, and also as in the Hieronymus. Who was never to be called Thomas Jefferson or Jerry Jefferson and certainly not Tee Jay as in Tee Jay period, but who was often called the Snake as in Snake Doctor and sometimes by extension Doctor Snakeshit, to wit, Shakespeare, the author of as many quotations as Anonymous himself! If you were known as snakeshit on the campus in those days, you were obviously somebody for whom doing things as required by the book was a snap, and who could talk as if sounding like a book was the most natural thing in the world.

But even as he used to say yea verily and reach for his notebook to record the goods on something, the T. Jerome Jefferson that I had recognized from the very outset as the best of all possible roommates ever and who was now almost a full year's long since long gone to other encounters elsewhere, always sounded to me as if as far as he was concerned, anything that was to be found in books, especially schoolbooks, even the most advanced schoolbooks, was not unlike the data on timetables, maps, and mileage charts. *Elementary, my dear Watson. Elementary.*

XXI

All the way out from the campus that Thursday evening the main thing on my mind was the stack of Louis Armstrong and Duke Ellington recordings that Hortense Hightower and I had pulled out and started playing the week before. Beginning with "When It's Sleepy Time Down South," we had spent all of the first hour listening to such Armstrong instrumentals as "Potato Head Blues," "Weary Blues," "West End Blues," "Weather Bird," "Beau Koo Jack," and "Struttin' With Some Barbecue" among others, each of which had become an instant standard as soon as shipments of it arrived at music stores and the record counters of department stores all over the country.

Then we had moved on to "Stardust," the national brown-skin dance-hall anthem since my junior high school days, "Lazy River," "I'm Confessin'," "When You're Smiling," and "Swing That Music" on which his epoch, yes epoch-making vocals were either matched or exceeded by his solo trumpet choruses. So then there were all of those recent show tunes like "Thanks a Million,"

"It's Wonderful," "I Double Dare You," "I'm in the Mood for Love," and so on, which made all pop singers want to sing like him from then on.

That took us up to the last fifteen minutes and we closed out with Armstrong taking the vocal and trumpet choruses on his band's version of Ellington's "Solitude," followed by Ellington's playing his own instrumental arrangement of his "Sophisticated Lady," which to this very day still takes me back to the way things used to be between me and the girls at Mobile County Training School between the ninth grade and the year I graduated and left town.

There was only enough time for one more then and since we had finally made it to the Ellington stack, we wrapped things up with a preaudition of the next week by playing "It Don't Mean a Thing if It Ain't Got That Swing," which I then whistled along with "Swing that Music" and Armstrong and the Red Onions' "Cake Walkin' Babies from Home" all the way back to the dormitory.

I already knew what my first selection was going to be and I had started whistling it as I came through the red-brick columns of the Emancipation Memorial Archway with the crown of three rings. It was "Echoes of Harlem," which was also called "Cootie's Concerto" because it featured Cootie Williams *(who was from Mobile!)* but which I liked just as much for the striding piano and bass fiddle figure that also made me think of it as a nocturne that was a perfect movie soundtrack for uptown hep cats on the prowl from after-hours ginmills to the wee hours key clubs along patent leather avenues.

Of course, there was also Ellington's music about the atmosphere of Harlem by day or night such as "Harlem Speaks," "Uptown Downbeat" and "I'm Slapping' Seventh Avenue with the

Sole of My Shoe"; and there were other concertos such as "Barney's Concerto" also known as "Clarinet Lament," and for Rex Stewart's cornet there was "Boy Meets Horn," and for the alto of Johnny Hodges there was "Sentimental Lady" among many others.

As I came on toward the point where the paved sidewalk used to end in those days, I was whistling and humming my way through passages that I already knew from "Hip Chic," "Buffet Flat," "Jazz Potpourri," "Battle of Swing," and "Slap Happy," but from time to time in spite of myself I couldn't keep myself from wondering what she had in mind when she said she was playing around with the idea of making me a proposal that she was almost certain was going to surprise me. So I had to remember to pace myself and not get there ahead of time.

But as soon as she let me into the darkened hallway, I could tell that somebody else was already there and that something else was already happening.

Well, here's that schoolboy right on the dot, she said. And I said, As scheduled. I said, Never is to be no CPT for me, Miss Boss Ladee, and she said, Come on back this way, and I followed her to the end of the hall and down the steps to what turned out to be the toilet for the basement party area, and that is when I saw Will Spradley for the first time.

Naked to the waist and with a towel around his shoulders like a shawl, he was sitting crossways on the closed toilet seat holding his bloody and swollen face over the washbasin, grunting and sighing and waiting for her, and she said, This is Will Spradley. He got himself all tangled up in a mess that looks like it might get bigger before it's over. So come on over here and help me with this, she said, and handed me a bottle of witch hazel, a vial of Mercurochrome, a package of gauze bandages, and a roll of tape from the cabinet behind the mirror above the basin and went on doing what she was doing to his face and head with the washcloth and towel, and that's when the phone rang upstairs.

So I took over while she went back up the stairs to the entrance hallway to answer it, and I saw the gashes and knots and puffs on his head and face and the bruises on his arms and torso, and every time he had to make any movement he grunted, and when he was not gasping from sudden stabs of sharp pain he was sighing and mumbling to himself, saying mostly the same thing over and over, answering his own questions as if the right words would undo what had happened. Unh unh unh, just look at all this now. Just look at it. You ever seen anything like this in your life? I know good and well I ain't never seen nothing like this in all of my born days. I swear to God. All of this and what did I do? I ain't done nothing. I ain't done nothing to nobody.

When she came back, she led him out to the couch near the small crescent-shaped bar in the party room where, along with an upright piano, a regular professional rockola, and a console radio, there as also a stack of folded bridge tables and chairs, a big round poker table, and a pool table.

That was him, she said. He's on his way but there's something else he's got to attend to first, and Will Spradley said, I got to see him because I got to tell him, because God knows I wasn't trying to get him in no trouble like this, and she said, Take it easy, Will, we know that; and Will Spradley said, All I was doing was what I was supposed to do and I just happened to run into Gile and that's what I told Dud Philpot and that's all I told him because I wasn't trying to get nobody in no trouble. That's how come I come on out here. Because I didn't want nobody to see me going back out to the Pit, and she said, He knows that, Will. She said, I called him as soon as you made it out here.

All I was trying to do was what I was supposed to be doing and now look at all this, Will Spradley said. I declare before God, he moaned, touching his back and sides with his swollen left hand

and pressing the cold damp folded face towels to his mouth and nose as I passed them to him while she went on trying to patch up his gashes and bruises using the Mercurochrome for some, Band-Aids for others, and gauze bandages for the larger ones.

Man, just look at you, she said, so just tell me one thing. How in the hell did you go and get yourself all tied up with some old poor white trash bloodsucker like Dud Philpot in the first goddamn place? You got to know better than that, Will Spradley, and he said, I don't know, Boss Lady. I just don't know, and she said, You hear this stuff, Schoolboy. As for myself, I still haven't been able to figure out how some of our people live to get to be as old as they do. It's a goddamn mystery to me how they don't poison themselves to death through just plain old dumbness.

Wait a minute, just a minute, just a minute, she said then and went over to a closet and came back and said, Here, help him into this, and handed me a faded blue-and-gray plaid sport shirt and put an old worn golf jacket on the chair by the couch. The shirt was size forty-two. Will Spradley was about size forty, but he was just about six feet even, and he must have weighed about a hundred and eighty-five lean hard pounds. I didn't know what Dud Philpot looked like then, but later I found out that he was in his early fifties and was about five-eleven and weighed about a hundred and forty-some bony-butt stooped-shouldered perpetually restless pounds.

I want you to know how much obliged I am to you for this you doing for me, Miss Boss Lady, Will Spradley said. I really do, he said, and I never will forget it as long as I live, he said, and she said, Which thanks to all this mess you now got us all in may not be all that long. And he said, Consarn the luck. I know it, Miss Boss Lady, and that's what bothers me more than anything else and that's exactly why I come all the way over here trying to warn Gile.

And Don't think I don't appreciate that either, she said, and then she said, Look, I hate to be fussing at you like you ain't already got troubles enough, Will Spradley, but goddamn man, there are white folks and there are white folks and you been around long enough to know what kind of white folks Dud Philpot is. Dud Philpot come from some of them old backwoods rosin-chewing razorback peckerwoods. Any fool ought to be able to see that, Will Spradley, she said, and then she said what she also said about knowing that class of white people once person-to-person. Because, if your folks and their folks have been knowing each other for a while, that made all the difference in the world and you turned each other favors and country folks to country folks regard-less of being on different sides of the color line when you came into town.

But if you were just another one of us trying to transact business with one of them that you don't know, they can excuse themselves for anything they do against you. From cheating to lynching. Because all they have to remember is that in spite of the fact that their white skin is supposed to put them above you, even the slaves back on the old plantations were better off than their so-called free but often raggedy-assed and half-starved and mostly despised foreparents.

You're right, Miss Boss Lady, Will Spradley said. Cain't nobody dispute that because here he comes jumping me like that after all them weeks and months I been meeting them time pay-ments. You sure right because I feel like a fool for being surprised and now just look at all this trouble I might be causing all of us. That's how come I'm trying to find Gile. Because it's all my fault and I know it now and maybe it's too late.

I was listening and trying to put the situation together as well as I could and as fast as I could, and at first the problem was that I thought that Will Spradley was somebody who worked at the club or maybe at the Pit and then I had thought maybe Will Spradley was in such a hurry to see Giles Cunningham because he needed to borrow money to pay off an overdue debt to Dud Philpot, whoever Dud Philpot was, and then I realized that I had already become that much a part of something about which I didn't yet really know anything at all.

I sure do hope Gile hurry up and get here because I got to see him and tell him, Will Spradley said, because I don't want him thinking I'm like that because I know what people always subject to say and it ain't fair because it ain't true because I might be poor and sometimes I might have to take low and pick up what I can but I ain't no white man's nigger. I don't care what nobody say. I ain't never done nothing against my own.

He know Gile, Will Spradley went on talking as much to himself as to me and the Boss Lady. He got to know Gile. Everybody know Gile Cunningham, and everybody know Gile Cunningham ain't never about to be giving in to no Dud Philpot, so then here he come buck-jumping at somebody like I'm the one when all I'm doing is standing around out there waiting for him so I can straighten up with him and get on about my business.

Then the three of us were just sitting there, waiting as if for the next weather report as you did when you were down on the Gulf Coast during hurricane season, and that was when Hortense Hightower asked him if he felt well enough to fill me in on what the situation had added up from. She said I was her young friend from the campus, and he said, Sure because I'm the onliest one that can tell it to you just exactly the way I got myself all tangled up in all this mess like this. Sure, because maybe you the kind of college boy that can see my point, like I'm counting on Gile doing. Because he the one I'm counting on. Sure, because most of these other folks ain't no better than white folks.

But he didn't begin at the beginning. He began at the point where he was coming along the railroad spur and was stopped by Giles Cunningham in a car being driven by Wiley Peyton, and as he went on talking and dabbing his nose and mouth with the face towel that he kept dipping into the basin of water on the stool in front of him, he recounted everything, not only word for word but sometimes also thought for thought and almost breath for breath. So much so that it was not only as if you were an eye and ear witness but also the actual participant himself.

Maybe it was because I just couldn't stop thinking about the music I had come to play on the phonograph that evening. Maybe so, maybe no. But as closely as I was following every detail of the story Will Spradley was retelling, not only for my benefit but also for his own, as soon as he started telling about it in his own way and at his own pace, it was also as if you were listening to an almost exact verbal parallel to one of the Ellington records that was near the very top of my list for that night. It was called "In a Jam," but not because it was a song with lyrics about being in trouble. So far as I know, there never were any lyrics. The chances are that it was so named because it was an instrumental composition derived from the interplay of voices in a jam session.

And yet, of its very nature as a piece of music, "In a Jam" was also about being in a tight spot. A jam session, after all, is a musical battle royal, and as such it is always a matter of performing not only with hair-trigger inventiveness and ingenuity but also with free-flowing gracefulness which is to say elegance, not only under the pressure of the demands of the music itself but also in the presence of and in competition with your peers and betters.

All of which also added up to making the jam session a matter of antagonistic cooperation that enriched the overall rendition even as it required each instrumentalist to perform at the very highest level of his ability. Such, as every jazz initiate knows, is also precisely how the jam session also serves to expose the fact that there are times when the personal best of some musicians is none too good. Not that such is the basic function of the jam session by any means. Originally it was simply of participating in a jamboree in celebration of something. Nor did anybody understand all of that more than did

Duke Ellington even back then the plaintive emphasis of whose score makes it all too obvious that in this instance he was more interested in the structure of the jam session as such than with what he was later to call the velocity of celebration.

In any case, it was as if Will Spradley's plaintive voice, which already sounded so much like Tricky Sam Nanton's plunger-muted trombone to begin with, was also by turns all of the hoarse ensemble shouts plus the sometimes tearful piano comps and fills of Duke Ellington himself as well as each solo instrument including the alto of Johnny Hodges, the clarinet of Barney Bigard, and so on through the call and response dialogue to the somewhat bugle/trumpet tattoo sound of Rex Stuart's cornet out-chorus solo that you heard every time he made any mention of Giles Cunningham.

When he came to the point where he made his getaway through the back door of Dudley Philpot's store, he stopped and just sat sighing and grunting and shaking his head and dabbing the cold towels to his nose and mouth again, and Hortense Hightower said, Man, goddamn. Man, look like you coulda done *something* to keep that bony butt son-of-a-bitch from kicking your ass like this. I swear to God, Will Spradley, I swear to God.

But all he would say then was, I just want Gile to hurry up and come on over here so I can tell him and explain my part to him because he the one all this is about and I don't care what these old other folks think because they going to say what they going to say about me anyhow. They don't want to know the truth. They just want to talk about somebody. But Gile is a businessman and he knows business is business and that's the way he is and that's what I like about him.

Well, just take it easy, she said. He'll be here in a little while. Just as soon as he can, she said. But goddamn, she said to me then, can you believe all this stuff you just been hearing, Schoolboy? Myself, I know damn well it sure the hell is happening, but I'm still having a hard time *believing* it.

XXII

You could tell that Will Spradley didn't really believe that it was really happening either. Even as he sat sighing and moaning and nursing his lacerations and closed eye, you could see that he was still expecting to wake up and find that all of the pain and breathless urgency was only a part of a very bad dream brought on by his worries about his money problems which, given just half a chance, he could explain his way out of for the time being.

But when Giles Cunningham finally made it there and filled us in on his part, you knew that he was not having any problem at all in believing in the consequences of what he had become caught up in several hours ago when Dud Philpot had come charging into the office out at the Pit, because all during the time he was talking to the three of us, he didn't miss a step or even pause in the preparations that he was making for his next move.

That was when I found out what he had been doing while I was helping Hortense Hightower give first aid to Will Spradley. She had called him as soon as Will Spradley had showed up, saying what he was saying, and he had clued in Speck Jenkins at the Pit, Wiley Peyton at the Dolomite, and Flea Mosley out at the Plum, and then he had headed over to Gin Mill Crossing to the poker game in Yancey William's club room, because that was where he could find most of the help he was counting on, and when he pulled into the yard and saw the other cars he knew that most of the friends he was looking for were there already.

Big Bald Eagle Bob Webster opened the door and reached out to slap-snatch palms and stood grinning his ever-so-playful but ever-so-steady, bald-eagle-eyed, scar-cheeked grin at him with the others acknowledging his arrival without really looking up from the tobacco-copy, corn whiskey, cozy pomade-plus-after-shave, cozy hum-and-buzz at the green-felt-cushioned poker-round table.

Hell yeah, it's him all right, Bald Eagle Bob Webster, whom some called Eag and others called Bar-E, said. Grady MacPherson, who was holding the deck, said, Yeah, come on in here, man, goddamn; and Eugene Glover said, Hey, goddamn right, come on in here. Hey, where you *been*, man? And Felton Carmichael said, Hey that's all right about where the hell he been. Just bring your old late self on into this old chicken-butt house now, cousin.

He had stepped inside but he still stood where he was and waited with his hand up. The others, some sitting around the table as players, others hovering around, some only as onlookers and others waiting a turn—or the right moment—were Solomon Gatewood, Logan Scott, Eddie Rhodes, Curtis Howard, and Wendell Franklin, who said, Man, pull off your coat and money belt, and Logan Scott said, Hey, we been waiting for you, man.

So come on in here with all that money, man, Curtis Howard said, and Grady MacPherson said, All that *long* money, man, and Solomon Gatewood said, Come on in here with all of *my* money, man, and somebody else said, Man, come on in here with all of *all of our* money, and nobody noticed that he was standing with his hand up because they were all so busy signifying at him and laughing among themselves without interrupting the deal going down at the same time that nobody had turned to look at him as yet.

Old money himself in person, Logan Scott said back over his shoulder, still watching the table, Come on money, and Wendell Franklin said, No, man, you talking about *Mister* Money. Come on *Mister* Money. And Curtis Howard said, Hey, wait y'all. What's this cat doing coming over *here* at *all?* With all the money he already got, this ain't nothing but some little old nickel-and-dime stuff to him. And Eddie Rhodes said, Man, that just goes to show you about money people. Now me and you just trying to pick up a little extra change because it will come in handy, but Old Giles Cunningham just like to be *around* money, even if it ain't nothing but a little *chickenshit chicken feed* like this. And somebody else said, No, man, Old Giles Cunningham like to have money *around him,* and Eddie Rhodes said, Hey, yeah man, that's a good one—*right around his waist.*

They were all laughing, and you couldn't help laughing at yourself with them, and you knew that they knew as well as you did that all of you always came together whenever you could, mainly because you always had such a good time just being together. Not that at least a little playful wagering was set almost always as part of it. Indeed, even when they were all emotionally aligned on the same side of some contest. They were likely to make side bets on specific aspects of the performance, such as point speed, extra points, home runs, extra base hits, strikeouts, or knockouts, round-by-round point tallies and so on. But obviously such petty wagering was always far more a matter of ceremonial risk-taking and sportsmanship than of making a killing. Clearly the main reason that they used to make such a big deal of getting together to listen to the radio broadcasts of the important prize-fights and the World Series and the Rose Bowl Game back in those pretelevision times was that it was the next best thing to sitting together at ringside or in the grandstand.

So what say, Giles, Logan Scott said, come on in the house, and Wendell Franklin said, Man, ain't you got that money belt off yet, and that was when they all finally turned to look at him and saw his hand up even as he laughed along with them, and that was when he said, Hey wait a minute, y'all. I trying to say something. Bald Eagle Bob Webster said, Hey Ho(ld) y'all. Hold on, hold on, hold on. He stood fanning his hands across each other in front of him and then he cocked his ear and said, Hey, what is it Giles? What's the matter, man?"

Hey, I'm sorry I'm late, y'all, he said, but looks like somebody got another kind of little game that just might be shaping up out there tonight. It might be just a threat, he said, but you never know, and that was when he told them about what had happened between him and Dudley Philpot out at the Pit that afternoon and about what Hortense Hightower had told him on the telephone about Will Spradley.

So now I guess it's supposed to be my turn if I'm still here after he told me to unass the area, he said, and Eugene Glover said, Giles, you mean to tell me that Dud Philpot told you that? Not Dud Philpot, Giles. Man, you can't mean some weasly clodhopper like Dud Philpot think he can come up with some old tired-ass peckerwood shit like that. Man, come on. And Bald Eagle Bob Webster said, Just tell us what the fuck you need, Giles, and you got it, man, you know that.

They were all waiting then and he said, Well, Eag, I could use some of y'all over at the Pit with Speck and some others over at the Dolomite with Wiley, and I got a couple of other things I got to see to by myself, and Yancey Williams said, Well, you just go on, Giles. You just leave that to me and Eag. We'll divide them up. You get to Speck, Eag, and I'll get to Wiley. And look, Giles, if a gang of them happen to jump you out there somewhere, all you got to do is make it on back over here. Hell, you know goddamn well ain't none of them going to try to follow you over in here.

Man, Bob Webster said, you couldn't *pay* none of some somitches to come over in here even before they got taught that lesson. I'm quite sure they'll never forget when they let some fool talk them into going up on the campus that time.

Everybody there remembered what had happened (and had not happened!) back some fifteen years earlier when the Ku Klux Klan was on the rise again for a while, following the World War in France. Some could tell you about it from first-hand experience and others had heard about it from somebody who had been either personally involved in one way or another or were around at the time. But the account of it that I have always been most familiar with is the one that Deke Whatley used to recount in the barbershop when he used to get going again on one of his first-chair sermons on the folly of political action without organization.

Anybody think I'm just talking about some kind of old church membership politics already missed my point, he always used to say. I ain't talking about nothing where you got to go to meeting and they collect dues for some sanctimonious hustler in a Cadillac to rake in. *Hey, remember that time when a bunch of them Old Ku Kluxers put on all of them sheets and shit and come talking about they going to bring a motorcade through the campus to show niggers that white folk mean for them to stay in their place? Well, gentlemen, the whole goddamn crew of them goddamn drunk-ass rednecks were all the way onto the grounds before it finally hit their dumb-ass asses that they hadn't seen a soul, not because everybody was either up there hiding under the bed or peeping out from behind the curtains, but because there were all of them combat-seasoned AEF veterans in the student body at that time and they and the ROTC cadets were all deployed in them hedges and behind them knolls and on top of them buildings, all them goddamn sharp-shooters and bayonet fighters and ain't no telling what else, gentlemen. Sheeet, them goddamn crackers got on the hell on through here in a hurry, then, and went on out somewhere and found themselves a hill and burned a chickenshit cross and went on back home and went to bed. Now that's what I'm talking about when I'm talking about organization. Them white folks said, Oh shit, these niggers up here* organized! *Let's get the hell out of here. And now that brings me to another point. Did you ever notice whenever some white folks go somewhere to pull some old shit like that and you let them get away with it, you going to see it all over the papers, and here comes all them old reporters from up north, can't wait to feel sorry for us and ain't going to do a damn thing to help out. But when some of us turn the goddamn tables on them somitches, all them newspapers act like ain't nothing at all happened in the first goddamn place. That's some more stuff I been studying for years and you know what I found out? I think them somitches know what they doing. Gentlemen, if they had put anything in the papers about how these folks had them people scared shitless because they were organized and just watching and waiting like that, it's subject to drive white folks crazier than the Brownsville raid, and ain't nobody fired one single round of nothing.*

I also remember him saying what he always used to say about Gin Mill Crossing he used to get going about how the main thing in that connection was to let *them* know that you ain't going to take no shit lying down! *And y'all know good and damn well I ain't talking about getting up somewhere woofing at somebody. You know me better than that. I'm talking about just letting them get the goddamn message that it's going to cost them something because you willing to put your ass on the goddamn line. Otherwise, here they come with some old foolishness like it's their birthright to make niggers jump. But now you take them people over in Gin Mill Crossing. Old bad-assed Cat Rogers himself don't go messing around over in there without first off giving somebody some advance notice, and he's the high sheriff and a tough somitch by any standard. Even if Cat want to get somebody that everybody already knows broke the law and got to go to jail, Cat always going to call Yank Williams or Big Eag, and they'll either say come on in or we'll send him out or he ain't here, and that's good enough for Cat Rogers. That's what I'm talking about when I'm talking about Gin Mill Crossing, gentlemen.*

So you just go on and take care of whatever you got to see to, Yancey Williams said outside on the porch with Bob Webster standing by as the others filed past, some still putting on their coats. Ain't going to take nobody here more than fifteen or twenty minutes to go by home and pick up what they need. What you think, Eag? and Big Bald Eagle Bob Webster said, probably no more than a quarter of an hour at most, and then goddamn it, we'll find out. But frankly, Giles, I can't see very many of them people following Dud Philpot nowhere. Maybe a few of them old razorbacks that been used to ganging up on somebody ten to one and saying shoo.

XXIII

This is my young friend from the campus I was telling you about, Hortense Hightower said when Giles Cunningham finally got there, and he said, What say there, my man? and I said, Nice to meet you, and we shook hands and he gave me a pat on the shoulder and turned to Will Spradley and said, Man, goddamn, just look at you, goddamn! Man, you let a nothing-ass somitch like Dud Philpot do something like this to you? Goddamn man. And Will Spradley said, That's all right about me, Gile. I just been trying to make it to you so I can tell you he done all this to me because you the one he really working himself up about. And Giles Cunningham said, Well I appreciate that, Will Spradley, I really do.

Then, looking at me again, he said, and I also want you to know how much I appreciate you giving the Boss Lady a hand with all of this. But hold up for a minute and I'll be right with you and we can talk while I do what I got to do and get on back out of here.

He moved on over to the wall behind the bar and unlocked

the door to the walk-in closet and when he clicked on the light the first thing you saw was a rack of shotguns and rifles, and it took only a glance for me to see that there were 20-gauge pumps as well as single- and double-barrel breechloaders and that the rifles included a lever-action Winchester, a bolt-action Enfield, a magazine-fed Springfield, a .30-caliber carbine, and also a stack-barrel combination 410-gauge shotgun and a .30-caliber rifle called an over-and-under gun.

I could spot any of those in a matter of seconds anywhere, even in a dim light, because Little Buddy Marshall and I had learned how to fire and also how to fieldstrip every one of them by the time I was thirteen years old. After all, hunting, like fishing, was so much a part of everyday life in Gasoline Point back then that you didn't think much more about using guns and rifles (but not pistols!) than about any of the other workaday tools that you were always being warned to be careful about. Pistols, to be sure, were another matter altogether. Whether revolvers or automatics, they were always special, always redolent of nimble daring and expert doing and escaping and retaliating. But then, pistols had just about nothing to do with hunting in the first place.

Anyway, I already had the gun rack checked out even before I realized that I was doing it, but it was not until after he had signaled for Will Spradley to be taken to another room for the time being that he said, Hey, Poppa, I can use a little help with this. Then when he opened the footlockers, I saw that there were also three Thompson submachine guns, also known as Tommy guns. And I said, Chicago Typewriters because that was what we used to call the ones you saw (and heard!) in the gangster movies in those days, and I said, These are the very first *real* ones I've ever actually seen, and he said, One for each place, but just in case.

Just in case, he said, and only just in case. I mean, this stuff is strictly for the last resort, he said, and then he said, What I really think they're most likely to have in mind is to come out and scare somebody. So if that's it and they get to any one of my joints and find Eag and the boys or Yank and the boys waiting for them, I think that just might take care of that, because they didn't leave home to go to no battle. They just out to have themselves a little cheap fun, showing off. But since you never can tell when some of them are subject to get all carried away and start trying to burn some property and all that, I got to have this stuff on hand just in case. *But now here's my point. Don't nobody in these parts know I have my hands on no stuff like this but the Boss Lady, Wiley, Speck, Flea, Eag, and Yancey and now you and that's the way I got to keep it. You get the point? And I said, I sure do, and I did. All you had to do was imagine the type of newspaper headlines that would be featured from border to border and coast to coast:* ALABAMIANS MOWED DOWN IN WILD TOMMY GUN MASSA-CRE BY CRAZED, RAMPAGING BLACK RENEGADES.

I sure do, I said, and he handed me one of the submachine guns and picked up the other two and I followed him out through the back door and up the steps to where the cars were parked and I guessed that the two he was carrying which he put into the trunk of his Cadillac were for the Pit and the Dolomite and that the one he took from me and put into the trunk of the Oldsmobile was for Flea Mosley, out at the Plum. Then on the way back inside, he said, the Boss Lady thinks a hell of a lot of you, my man, and I always trust her judgment about people. So look, he said as we came back down the steps, I'm sending her out to Flea and I really would appreciate it if I could get you to go along riding shotgun for her.

We were all back in the game room again then, and he said, Hey now look now if you have some concern about getting yourself in trouble with the school authorities, I can understand that. And I said, I'll take my chances. And we both knew that it was not just a manner of speaking what with the general campus discipline and specific dormitory rules being what they were in those days, and he said, See there, she knew she could count on you. Boy, this

woman's got judgment about people like old James P's striding left
hand. *She don't hardly ever miss.*

She herself was still working on Will Spradley's face and all
she did was look up and give me a wink that was not a part of her
nightclub Boss-Lady-at-the-microphone come-ons, and that was
when Giles Cunningham put the clip in the .38 automatic and
handed it to me along with the carbine and the musette bag
containing a supply of .30- and .38-caliber cartridges. Then he also
gave me a wink and feinted a left jab and went on getting ready
to go.

I could already see myself in the right front seat beside her
with the blue-steel automatic in my hand and the carbine on my
lap and the musette bag on the floor between my feet, but before
I had a chance to start trying to figure out all of the what-ifs and
what-if-nots you had to be ready for, Will Spradley started talking
again.

I had to make it to you, Gile, he said, because you the one
he really got it in for, Gile, he said, because he came lighting into
me like this, and took it out on me just because I was there when
he got back from out there and didn't get nowhere with you by
himself and he working himself up to get a bunch of them to come
at you. Now that's what happen, Gile, and that's how come I'm
here. Because if I was one to try to turn it on you just to get it off
of me, I wouldn't be here, Gile. I'd be out there trying to get long
gone somewhere from this whole place and never come back.

Hey like I said, Giles Cunningham said, I appreciate your
concern, Poppa, but don't worry about it. That somitch is mad with
me because of what happened when he came out to the Pit. But
Will Spradley said, Yeah, Gile, but I'm the one told him about you
cashing my check and that's how come he made it his business to
come out there like that, and if they find that out they going to say
that makes me a white man's nigger. Because I know these folks,
Gile, and Giles Cunningham said, Hey, take it easy man. What the

hell else could you tell him? You just told him the goddamn truth. Cain't nobody blame you for that. I sure the hell don't.

But you know these folks, Gile, Will Spradley said then. I mean, some of these folks. They get a hold of something like this and there they go, putting the bad mouth on somebody and making somebody a white man's nigger and don't know nothing about it, not a thing in the world. They going to say I'm that because I ought not to told him nothing. But that don't make me that, Gile. Because I may be poor and got to take low sometimes, but that don't make me no white man's nigger. Because I ain't never tattled nothing on none of us to none of them folks. Never in all of my born days.

I know what you mean, man, Giles Cunningham said, pulling on a single-breasted olive drab three-quarter-length raglan twill topcoat and gathering up the rifles and handguns he had come for. But come on now, man. I got to get on out of here and find out what these goddamn peckerwoods going to be trying to do. You go with the Boss Lady and the schoolboy.

Outside I took the shotgun seat and Will Spradley got into the back, and as we pulled out of the yard ahead of the Cadillac and headed for the secondary road that would take us to the route to the Plum Thickets, Will Spradley said, I never will forget you, Boss Lady, and I want to thank you again for giving me a chance to tell Gile. And then he said, Because the thing about the whole thing is that it ain't about nothing. Some little old percent that ain't nothing but some pennies and nickels and dimes. All of this about something like that and it ain't nothing.

She didn't cut in while he was talking but as soon as he paused she said, Later for that, Will Spradley. What we got to do now is stay quiet and keep our eyes and ears open.

XXIV

Augustus Strickland, *né* Edward Augustus Strickland II, was somebody I had been hearing about if only incidentally from the very outset of my freshman year. Indeed, unless you came onto the campus by automobile from Montgomery Fork as most students in those days did *not*, Strickland was a name you probably heard on the very same day you arrived, because the old antebellum mansion with its fluted columns and red-trimmed octagonal tower, concrete-patched trees, and wrought-iron fence called the Old Strickland Place and sometimes also referred to as Strickland Acres was the first thing you saw as soon as you came into the elm-lined curve less than a quarter of a mile beyond which was the entrance to the administration and academic end of the campus.

The first time I ever saw him in person, however, was one bright and breezy afternoon during the early part of that first November while I was standing on the corner by the Farmer's Exchange Bank. I heard somebody say, *Gus Strickland. There he is. Gus Strickland ain't but the one,* and I looked back across the street to the square and saw him getting out of the Cadillac convertible that I had just seen pulling up to one of the diagonal parking spaces facing the Confederate monument, and as he headed toward the courthouse wearing a tan-and-green houndstooth-check sport jacket, olive green open-collar knitted shirt, tan whipcord slacks, highly polished jodhpurs and a tan porkpie hat with the brim turned down all around. I remember thinking that he looked as much like a retired British army officer as like the rich Southern sportsman that he was—to whom business matters were mostly handled as if they had long since become more occasional and incidental than a part of his daily routine.

As a matter of fact, he had been a colonel in the AEF and probably still was a colonel if not a brigadier general in the Army Reserve Corps. But nobody ever addressed him or referred to him as Colonel Strickland, the Colonel, or certainly not the Old Colonel (which many people, by the way, used to seem to think meant not one who commands a regiment but one who owns an antebellum mansion and what was left of an antebellum plantation).

He was addressed by local white people as Mister Strickland, and by local Negroes as Mister Gus, but they thought of him and referred to him as Ole *Gus,* which was not to say *Old* Gus or *Old Man* Gus, but rather the legendary Gus that you've been long hearing tell of, which was entirely consistent with the fact that as often as not, any time you heard anybody say Gus Strickland, it was just about always as if what was being referred to was not unlike some elemental sociopolitical force that could probably be expressed in relative degrees to the nth power.

By the time I saw him on his way to the courthouse that afternoon, I already knew that he was the sole owner and proprietor of the Old Strickland Place and also that he didn't live there anymore. When he came back from the AEF, he had married a woman from Savannah and moved into another mansion, which I was not to see until sometime during the following summer and then only from a distance, but which was out beyond the south side of town and was said to have two tennis courts, a swimming pool, a man-made lake for fish and waterfowl, a stable for riding horses, and kennels for hunting dogs.

I was also to find out that he traveled a lot, not just from border to border and coast to coast, but also overseas. It was easy enough to imagine him in New Orleans for Mardi Gras, in Louisville for the Kentucky Derby, in Virginia for the fox-hunting season, and down in the canebrakes on the Gulf Coast for duck season, and also out in the Gulf Stream for deep-sea fishing. But he and his wife and two youngest daughters were also said to spend several months every other year or so traveling in Europe or the Middle East, and he was also known to have been across the Pacific to Hawaii and the Far East more than once.

Not that I ever had any special and certainly not any specifically personal reason to concern myself with what was going on in the life of Augustus Strickland. Nor had I done so. But on the other hand, he was not somebody that you would not know about or not have any more than a casual or incidental interest in either, anymore than you were likely to have only a passing curiosity about the Old Strickland Place itself. *Even those ever so much better off than thou and ever so deliberately incurious students from up north whose admitted fear of being down south was such that the very sound of a white Southerner's drawl seemed to make them feel as if being on the campus was, if anything, even worse than being foreign legionnaires in a remote desert outpost surrounded by murderous tribesmen wearing hooded sheets instead of burnooses, even they usually turned out to know exactly who he was, by reputation if not by sight. Whenever you heard another one of them saying, so that's Gus Strickland, there was always the same ring of familiarity but not the same overtone of outrage as when they said, So that's Cat Rogers, as if saying, So that's a rattlesnake.*

When you saw him on the campus, it was usually because he

had a standing invitation to head a local reception committee of his own selection to greet visitors of state, national, and international distinction. He was not and had never been a member of the board of trustees, because when the original Augustus Strickland had made the land available for the school's first campus, he had decided in accordance with his own personal policy for the reconstruction of freedmen as productive citizens, that in order for slaves to prove to themselves that they could manage their own affairs, no member of the Strickland family would ever serve in any official capacity on a board or any other committee established to formulate policy and supervise operations. And yet the attitude of the family over the years had always remained such that officials fully expected the school either to inherit the Old Strickland Place one day or be permitted to acquire it at a giveaway bargain.

Giles Cunningham knew what he knew about Augustus Strickland, not only as a local matter of course but also as information that had been of direct concern to him as a local businessman for almost ten years. It was, after all, from Augustus Strickland that he had begun buying up the adjacent lots as soon as the Pit had begun to catch on as a not-too-far way off campus roadside rib joint, and five years ago he had bought the property where the Club now was because Augustus Strickland, who knew that he was looking for a site to build a dance hall to book headline road bands into, gave him an inside tip on plans to turn that area beyond Montgomery Fork into several residential subdivisions and had made him a special bargain deal because the kind of classy college-oriented dance hall and night spot he was known to be planning would be a very attractive selling point that developers could use to entice home buyers to settle that far away from the campus.

There was, to be sure, the usual local down-home gossip,

speculation, and insinuation about which mulatto and light-brown-skin families may or may not have been blood relatives of this or that branch of the Strickland family of whichever generation. But nobody ever would have said that Giles Cunningham's special person-to-person business transactions with Augustus Strickland were connected in any way whatsoever with anything like that.

As far as Giles Cunningham himself was concerned, information about family bloodlines was not the sort of historical detail that mattered very much unless it had some direct bearing on obtaining clear title to a piece of real estate that he was negotiating to pick up. The relative purity or the degree of interracial mixture of family bloodlines as such was not something he bothered himself about at all. He just took it for granted that with the amount of passing for white he had come to know about over the years, most Americans, like it or not, admitted or not, come from an ancestry of mixed bloodlines.

It was usually as one businessman to another that he got in touch with Augustus Strickland, and once everything was in place that was also the way he felt about what he was doing when he called him and told him about Dudley Philpot that night, and when Augustus Strickland asked him if he had already called Cat Rogers, he said he had not and didn't intend to since he was not going to try to swear out any warrant against Dud Philpot.

I just wanted to touch base with you so that if this turns into some real trouble, you know my position, he said, and Augustus Strickland said, Hell, Giles, let me see if I can find out what the hell got into that damn Philpot and what he thinks he's up to and I'm going to have a word with Cat Rogers, too, Giles. After all, he's the high sheriff and somebody got to see it that he gets a reasonable chance to discharge his responsibilities.

I'm not about to be the one to try to dispute that, Giles Cunningham said then. I just don't want him to get that all mixed up with doing me some kind of personal favor and expecting me to be grateful for it.

I'll get right back to you as soon as I find out something, Giles, Gus Strickland said, and Giles Cunningham said, I appreciate that and I'll be right here at the Pit unless he turns up over at the Dolomite.

XXV

When we came through town, the streets around Courthouse Square were as empty as they usually were at that time of night. I didn't say anything, but I couldn't help wondering if that meant that trouble had already started out at the Pit or at the Dolomite or maybe even at both places. We circled around to the other side of the square and came on out along South Main Street to the city limits marker and through the outskirts and then we were on our way through the open country with the speedometer moving up to 50 mph and then 55 and beyond.

The bright head beams pushed on through the darkness as the windshield wipers clicked and clacked, swishing and swashing and squigging against the thin, steady, central Alabama early spring drizzle; and with Will Spradley still doubled up on the back seat and with Hortense Hightower handling the Oldsmobile exactly like the expert driver that I was to find out that she had already become all the way back during the earliest days of her apprenticeship in a two-car territory band out on the old southeast

198

vaudeville circuit, the only thing to do was keep on the lookout.

I was pretty sure that nobody was following us, but I also knew that any lights coming up from the rear could turn out to be a carload of drunken, self-indulgent white hell-raisers on their way back out of town after a showdown at the Pit, and there was also a chance that any traffic you met was on its way in to join the mob.

At that time, I was only somewhat familiar with the route we were following, so it was only from road maps of that part of Alabama that I could remember that the next town of any size was Junction Springs, which was all the way across the county line. I knew that we didn't have to go that far and, from the map, I also knew that if you did you could go on south by east to Eufaula and from there you could take the bridge across the Chattahoochee and be in Georgia. Or you could head due south again for the Florida panhandle by way of Dothan, from which you could also go to Jacksonville, by way of Valdosta, Georgia.

We came zooming on along the damp but unslippery black-top U.S. federal route and when you are traveling in mostly level farming country like that and there are no sharp curves and no other traffic, a steady sixty-five soon begins to feel like only forty-five, and if you start checking and rechecking your watch, you're almost certain to get the impression that time itself has slowed down.

Then there was the weatherworn country crossroads shack that I remember whenever I remember that part of that night, not because it represented any special landmark as such but because when I saw the milepost across from it and realized how far out beyond the town limits we had actually come, that was where and when I suddenly found myself missing the wee hour coziness of my dormitory room and becoming concerned about getting back into the also and also of the campus again.

Up to that point, I had been so completely caught up in the step-by-step urgency of the situation I had walked into and then also with being on hair-trigger alert for what I knew could happen next that it was as if I had somehow forgotten that I was really only a college boy with assignments in preparation and class sessions to attend the next day, beginning at nine o'clock with a lecture period to be followed by a break and lunch and then a session at two in the afternoon.

It was also as if I had forgotten that the also and also of the campus had come to include the also and also of the unfinished matter of one Miss Nona Townsend, a sophomore from Tuscumbia County by way of a freshman year at Alabama Normal, whom I had met back during the first week of that third October and to whom I had said what I said because she looked and moved and also sounded so much like the crepe myrtle–cape jasmine beautiful tea-cake perfect tan brown-skin storybook princess that I had always been looking forward to meeting and making myself worthy of some time later on along the way from the spyglass tree to the also and also of whatever wherever.

You could tell that she was used to having people say ingratiating things to her and as nice-mannered and appropriately modest as her responses always seemed to be, it was also easy enough to see that she was not somebody who really had very much patience with people who were preoccupied with good looks as such or with any of the other superficial values that their flattery suggested. So I didn't say what I said until I was reasonably sure that I could get away with it, and I did get away with it because by then I had smiled and said hello that many times without making a pass, because I wanted her to become curious enough to find out about me and not think that I was some fast-talking hotshot upperclassman on the prowl for innocent newcomers.

But I had not followed through. I had not really backed away either. But I had not followed up. Not because I had changed my mind. Not about her. There was nothing disappointing about her. The problem was that I still could not afford to have a steady girlfriend, because I just simply did not have the extra spending change that you had to have for the numerous essentials in the way of treats and favors you were expected to be able to provide when you went steady with somebody on campus in those days, and I had absolutely no intention of giving up any of my free reading time in the library and taking a part-time job in order to finance my social life. That would violate every promise I had ever made to get to college in the first place beginning back with Miss Lexine Metcalf before Mister B. Franklin Fisher and the Early Birds (knights of the ancestral imperative that they expected to be) and not excluding Miss Slick McGinnis.

And yet there she was as if custom-made, and the next moves were up to me. So I decided to take my chances, and hope that I would be lucky enough to get by with inviting her to go to only those on-campus entertainment events that were covered by the Student Privilege card. The idea was to make it through the rest of the term. Then I would have that last summer to pick up some extra cash for the social obligations of my senior year, and so far I had been able to get by because as a second-year transfer student concerned with making the smoothest possible academic transition from one campus to another, she had already restricted her availability for dates anyway.

You couldn't have asked for a better deal. It was indeed almost as if she herself had suggested that she would be busy doing whatever fairy-tale princesses always do in the castle while the as-yet untried and unproven apprentice knight-errant scoots hithering and thithering about, trying to forge his magic wandlike sword and get himself together to fulfill the mission that he had inherited because he is who he is and that will qualify him for an invitation to the castle.

But now as the Oldsmobile came zooming on further and further beyond the milepost at the crossroads shack, it was as if the main purpose of getting through the night and back onto the campus was to see her the next morning after my first class, when she would be coming down the stairway from room 201 where English Literature Survey Course 203 Section I was held. I wanted to be waiting at the drinking fountain just to say hello and be that close again and walk across the quadrangle with her to the library again.

Meanwhile, Hortense Hightower drove on, cruising between 55 and 60, and without taking her eyes from the road she winked and smiled every now and then to let you know that she was satisfied with the way things were going, but she had not said anything since she pulled out of her neighborhood, and she still didn't say anything until she began slowing down because we were coming to the turnoff. Then all she said was, Here we go, Will Spradley. You all right back there, Will Spradley? and Will Spradley said, I'll just say I'm still here, Boss Lady. I'll just say I'm still here.

She turned off and we came on into the woods and along a narrow winding downhill road to a clearing that was the parking area for the Club, and the first thing we saw was Flea Mosley waiting for us outside under the canopy to the main entrance, and when we pulled up, he said, You sure did get yourself on out here Boss Lady, but don't get out, don't even cut the motor. Giles wants y'all just to turn right on around and come right straight on back into town, and he say ain't nothing happening so don't worry about a thing. Ain't going to be no showdown because the peckerwoods ain't going to show up. Giles say just zip right on back in and drop the college boy on the campus and take Will Spradley on over to the school hospital and he also said find out what time the college boy can be down at the barbershop so Wiley or somebody can pick him up and bring him out to the Pit for lunch tomorrow and he will fill him in then. That's what the man said, Boss Lady, so don't let me hold y'all up no longer.

XXVI

So I didn't find out what had happened to make it all turn out the way it did until I heard about it directly from Giles Cunningham himself during lunchtime out at the Pit that next day. And that was also when he went on to say what he said about me and about a part-time summer job beginning the week after school was out at the end of May and lasting through the Labor Day weekend.

Dud Philpot had not carried out his threat, because within probably less than twenty minutes after Will Spradley had moved out of his reach and escaped through the back door and delivery alleyway, he himself had been taken to the emergency ward of the county hospital, where he was still in the intensive care unit under an oxygen tent (that I was to find out later, incidentally, could always count on emergency backup equipment and supplies from the infirmary on the campus).

To tell you the goddamn truth, Giles Cunningham said as he and Hortense Hightower and Wiley Peyton and I ate our soup and sandwiches, I never could see that many of the kind of white people we have around here letting themselves be rounded up and led anywhere by some baggy-britches redneck like Dud Philpot. But you never can tell. So when the Boss Lady called me and told me about Will Spradley turning up over there all beat up like that and worrying about me because I was the one Old Dud was really mad at, I figured I best not take no chances because even if he came back out here with just a couple of them old dirt-poor razorbacks from somewhere out there in that neck of the woods he come out of, ain't no telling what it could lead to before these people around here find out what it all started about. Because now let me tell you something. Don't ever forget how little it takes to set thousands of normal-seeming white people back not just to all of the old nightmares their foreparents on the plantation used to have about the slaves killing everybody in their sleep but on past that and all the way back to all of the panic the goddamn Indians used to cause among the early settlers. Man, you don't ever want to do anything that's going to make somebody realize how scared they are of you, especially when they happened to be the ones with most of the goddamn guns and know how to use them and don't mind using them. Look, you don't have to let nobody mess over you. But the minute you start going around trying to prove just on some kind of general principle that you ain't scared of them, you can get a lot of folks maimed and killed just because you got it all backward.

So anyway, that's why I also got in touch with Gus Strickland, he said, and I also knew that he would be the best one to find Cat Rogers and get him on the ball; and he called me inside of about ten minutes and told me what happened. Cat Rogers had just had the ambulance come to pick Dud Philpot up from the sidewalk where he had crumpled on the way from his store to the curb where his car was parked, and that's just about the story of how come the trouble didn't go any further than what he did to Will Spradley.

By the way, what about Will Spradley, Boss Lady? I said, and she said, I just circled back over by the campus hospital on my way over here and he's doing all right. They had to put in a few stitches but the way he's carrying on, when the time comes to take them out he intends to be somewhere up north with one of his cousins.

Hey, look my man, Giles Cunningham said reaching over and touching my arm, I really want you to know how much I appreciate what you did last night and when I said, But I didn't really do anything, he said, Don't play yourself cheap. You did plenty. Just falling in with us like that said a lot and the Boss Lady was telling me about how much confidence it gave her to have somebody out there with her acting like he knew what he might have to do. Man, she made you sound like somebody with the makings of just the kind of real pro that I'm always on the lookout for and she already been telling me about how much you like music.

Then he said if I needed a part-time summer job so that I could buy a couple of new outfits and also have some extra spending money for my senior year, all I had to do was let him know by the middle of May and by June we could work out something that I could take care of along with my own campus obligations to the Scholarship Award Program; and I said, I certainly would, and I also said, Absolutely, no doubt about it.

They were all smiling at me then, and when I said, I can't even begin to tell you how much this means, especially at this particular time, he said, You don't have to, and when I tried to thank him he said, Hey, I'm the one doing the thanking my man, and the thing about it is that it is really my privilege because I know damn well that what I'm offering you is just a little two-bit bonus that I know you can get along without, and I said, Yes but that's also what makes it so special.

As we went on talking, he wanted to hear about Mobile, and it turned out that I knew something about some of the downtown people he asked about and that he had also had business dealings with some that I had only heard about. Then while we were finishing our coffee, he lit a cigar and said, So here's my hand. The Boss Lady will get you back on the campus for your next class.

But when she and I came outside, I found that I had another surprise coming. Because when I saw the Oldsmobile there was the head of a bass fiddle case sticking out from the back seat, and she said that I was looking at what the proposition that we hadn't had time to get to last night was all about. She said, I changed my mind about something.

She said, This thing has been downstairs in the closet since I don't know when. Then one day not long ago when I got to thinking about how much more you always seem to hear on all those records we been spinning than most professional musicians I know, I said to myself, I bet you I already know exactly what would happen if he had this thing to play around with. Just for fun. So I said, I'm going to see, and so I had it fixed up for you. So you take it and you got the rest of this term and the whole summer and all of next term.

So that's my proposition, she said, and she said, All you got to do is get somebody in the string section of the Chapel Orchestra to give you a little start with a few rudiments and you'll be fingering and reading and figuring all kinds of stuff out for yourself in no time at all. Because you see, I already know how you whistle and hum along and how you don't just *keep* the time but also have to play around with it.

Which, she said, is exactly what made me change my mind. Because at first I was glad that you were not tied down to one instrument because you always listened to the whole band and not just for the place where your instrument comes in. But in this way I'm going to be able to hear you listening to everything all the time just like the drummer and like when the piano player is the one in charge like Duke and Count.

So what about it? she said as we came on by the old Strickland place and up the slope to that end of the budding green campus, and I said that I had never thought about it like that, and then I said, Never is to be one to not try, Boss Lady, never no days like that.

We were there then, and she let me out on the empty ramp to the front entrance to the dormitory, and I stood with my arms around the neck and shoulders of the bass fiddle and waved and watched as she pulled on off along the campus mainline and went on out of sight around the knoll across from the promenade lawn and then to the turn-off that passed the dormitory where the clock tower was.

Then before going to my afternoon seminar, I had to take the bass fiddle upstairs to 359, which since the beginning of June almost nine months ago I had been lucky enough to have all to myself as my own turret-tall spyglass tree above but never apart from the also and also of either the briar patch itself or any of the blue steel and rawhide routes hithering and thithering toward the possibility, however remote, of patent leather avenues in beanstalk castle town destinations yet to come.

About the Author

ALBERT MURRAY was born in Nokomis, Alabama, in 1916. He grew up in Mobile and was educated at Tuskegee Institute, where he later taught literature and directed the college theater. A retired major in the U.S. Air Force, Murray has been O'Connor Professor of Literature at Colgate University, visiting professor of literature at the University of Massachusetts in Boston, writer-in-residence at Emory University, and Paul Anthony Brick Lecturer at the University of Missouri. His other works include *The Omni Americans* and *The Hero and the Blues*, collections of essays; *South to a Very Old Place*, an autobiography; *Train Whistle Guitar*, a novel; *Stomping the Blues*, a history of the blues; and *Good Morning Blues: The Autobiography of Count Basie* (as told to Albert Murray). He lives in New York City.